IMMORTAL BILLIONAIRES BOOK 1

AFTER
I *Fall*

MELISSA SERCIA

AFTER I FALL
Immortal Billionaires, Book 1

Melissa Sercia
www.melissasercia.com

Cover Design by Sarah Paige. All stock photos licensed appropriately.

Edited by Katie Golding

Formatted by Champagne Book Design

For information on subsidiary rights, please contact the publisher at melissaserciawrites@gmail.com
Print Edition ISBN: 978-1-7358512-1-1
Printed in the United States of America

To Christopher
For always catching me when I fall...

IMMORTAL BILLIONAIRES BOOK 1

AFTER
I Fall

One

Raven

A PRETTY BLONDE GREETED ME WITH A WARM SMILE. SHE pulled me into an unexpected embrace. "You must be Raven! Welcome." Her rose scented hair brushed my cheek. It smelled expensive.

"Piper, nice to finally meet you in person. Thanks again for renting me a room." With just one glance into her luxury apartment, I already felt out of place. I was a long way from Maplewood. I had to keep reminding myself that it was a good thing. That small towns and first loves who break your heart were things better left behind.

New beginnings were like elevators, lifting you up and down. The doors slide open to give you a peek of each floor and close before you can linger too long. And when you did arrive at your destination, when you finally stepped out, the elevator would disappear behind the doors, becoming your past, and leaving you alone on the floor of new beginnings. Change wasn't always bad, but new didn't mean good either.

Piper ushered me in, helping me with my bags. "Where's the rest of your stuff?"

"It's…all I have. You said the room was furnished right?" Piper was from my hometown but everything about her screamed New York City. By the looks of the leather couch and fancy art on the walls, it was obvious she was doing well for herself.

"Of course. No worries. I'm such a hoarder, I just assume everyone is. Come, let me give you a tour of the place." Her recovery was flawless. She didn't even bat an eyelash at my hesitancy.

The kitchen was small but exquisite with its gas range stove and marble counter tops. I was already picturing all of the meals I could create here. The living room was huge with floor to ceiling windows overlooking the city, a leather couch, a glass coffee table covered in travel magazines, and a baby grand piano sat in the corner.

"Do you play?" I asked.

Piper shrugged as she chewed on the end of one of her pointy red acrylic nails. "I used to. I don't really have time for it anymore. How about you? You're welcome to play anytime you like."

I choked back a nervous laugh. "Oh, no. I don't have a musical bone in my body. My talents are in the kitchen."

"Well, when I'm actually home for more than twenty-four hours, you'll have to make something for me. I don't even know how to turn on the stove," she joked.

Piper led me down a short hall, stopping midway to show me the bathroom, a small but lavish room with thick white towels, colorful soaps, and one of those fancy rain shower heads that I've only ever seen in hotels. *I couldn't believe I was going to get to live here.*

At the end of the hall were three bedrooms—Piper's master suite with its own bathroom, a small office, and finally, what was to be my room. I gasped at the sight of it. It was bigger than my entire apartment in Maplewood. The furnishings were sleek and modern—minimalistic with muted gray tones and sharp lines. The king size bed was fitted with gray sheets and black throw pillows. The mattress sat upon a flat black bed frame with a short headboard that poked out from behind.

There was a small desk against the wall, a sitting area with what she called a *fainting couch*, and a vanity table framed by an enormous mirror. More of that fancy abstract art hung on the walls in between the two floor to ceiling windows. The room was so spacious, I could do cartwheels across the hardwood floor.

"Well, what do you think?" Piper asked.

"I'm speechless. Are you sure you're charging me enough? Not that I'm complaining." I couldn't really afford to pay more, but I didn't want her to feel like she was getting cheated either.

She tossed her silky blond hair over her shoulder, showcasing a tiny black heart tattooed on her collarbone. "Nonsense. Money is not a concern. I'd much rather help out a fellow Maplewood and know my apartment is in trusting hands when I'm gone. I still can't believe we are only now just meeting for the first time."

Maplewood was a small town. Everyone knew everybody. Except for a few of the elite rich girls who chose to pretend the rest of us didn't exist. I didn't have the heart to tell her that we had met before, she was just too popular to remember a nobody like me.

"Well, thank you for letting me stay here."

Piper grinned wide, revealing the whitest and straightest teeth I'd ever seen. "I'll let you get settled in. I've got to run to the airport. My flight leaves in three hours. There's food in the fridge and wine in the cabinet. Please, help yourself to both. I should be back in a few weeks, but I left you an emergency contact list on the kitchen table in case you need anything."

It was strange. I had just gotten here and the only person I knew in New York was leaving town. I was already nervous about being out of my comfort zone, now I'd have to get used to being alone more too. "What is it you do exactly?" I realized I didn't even know what she did for a living.

Piper fiddled with one of her diamond earrings, averting her gaze toward the window. "Oh a little bit of everything. It's pretty boring actually. But I love the traveling. That's the best part, seeing the world."

A twinge of jealousy rippled through me. Other than now, and one summer spent abroad after high school graduation, I hadn't really been anywhere else. Traveling was expensive and the Maplewood Diner barely paid me enough to cover my bills. If it weren't for that culinary internship and the winery paying my way there, I wouldn't have made it to Italy either. There were so many places I still dreamed of visiting. So many types of cuisine I wanted to master around the world.

"That sounds exciting. Where are you off to this time?"

Piper shrugged. "Don't know yet. They'll tell me when I get to the jet center. Speaking of which, I need to get going. Welcome to New York, Raven." She winked and sauntered out, leaving me alone in my gigantic room to unpack. Jet center? Her boss must be loaded if she's flying on a private jet.

Thirty minutes later, I heard the wheels of a suitcase rolling across the hardwood floor, and Piper calling out, "Bye Raven! See you in a few weeks." The door clicked and locked behind her before I could respond.

After putting all my clothes away, I wandered back into the front room. I found the wine she had been referring to and was impressed with her collection. I picked out a French Bordeaux and sipped it by the window. The sky was the color of orange sherbet and the lights across the city were beginning to flicker on. It took my breath away. *I could get used to this.*

I wondered if Piper had anyone to share this view with. It was as picturesque as views could be. Like straight out of a Monet painting. I was suddenly more aware of my loneliness than I usually allowed myself to be. Alex would have loved this view. *Just not with me.* Not anymore.

I rubbed my temples as a searing pain took hold above my eyebrows. Another damn migraine. I never used to get stress headaches before. Not until… *Ugh don't go there right now, Raven.*

I rummaged around in the fridge and realized by *food*, Piper meant cheese and bread. I was too tired to figure out who to order delivery from so I made a cheese sandwich, polished off another glass of wine and got ready for bed. I needed to find a job tomorrow so I couldn't drink the whole bottle no matter how badly I wanted to.

My drugstore products seemed even cheaper and more tacky sitting on the counter in Piper's designer bathroom. I brushed my teeth, scrubbing the red wine stains off, and crawled into bed. The sheets were the softest fabric I'd ever felt against my skin. The pillows lush and comforting. After the long bus ride, and the stress of moving, it didn't take long for me to drift off to sleep.

❧

The light blinded me awake and for a second I forgot where I was. I staggered up, cursing at myself for forgetting to close the enormous black-out drapes before I passed out last night. But considering I had also forgotten to set my alarm, it turned out to be a blessing. I dragged my feet out of bed and into the bathroom. My black hair was a tangled mess which meant I'd have to wash it and blow dry it out straight if I wanted to look presentable today.

Shit! It wasn't until I peeled back the shower curtain and turned on the hot water that I realized I had forgotten to pack my shampoo. I hesitated and considered checking out Piper's bathroom for some. She did say to make myself at home. And I would replace what I used.

I crept into Piper's master suite like a little kid snooping through their parent's bedroom. Even though she didn't *say* to stay out of her room, I still felt guilty traipsing through her private space. But whatever. I needed to wash my hair so I didn't look like I just crawled out of a forest.

Her room was even more luxurious than mine if that was even possible. In the center of the room sat a large four poster bed that looked like something out of a medieval castle. Out of the corner of my eye, I spotted wrist restraints, hanging off the headboard. Hmm, *kinky Piper.*

I felt my cheeks flush even though no one was in the room to judge me. I jerked my head away and headed straight for her bathroom. I let out a gasp at the sight of it. Next to an enormous jetted jacuzzi tub, was an equally large shower complete with a love seat and two shower heads—one on either side. *Who needs two shower heads?*

The minute I thought it, I wanted to take it back. *Someone who actually has someone to shower with, of course.* I was so naïve sometimes. Alex and I never took showers together. We barely had sex with the lights on. A faint pressure started to press on my brow. *Ugh, not again.* Just the mere thought of him sent my body into mass anxiety and distress. I needed to get the shampoo and get out of there.

I spotted a sleek bottle, snatched it up, and sprinted out of there, closing the door behind me so I wouldn't be tempted to wander back in. After a long hot shower, makeup, and blow out, I put on my best "interview" outfit and gave myself another once over in the mirror. And I wanted to cringe. In a small town, I turned heads, but after seeing Piper and her designer clothes and perfectly manicured nails, I had a feeling that wasn't going to be the case here. Looking at my drab gray pantsuit and white polyester blouse made me want to jump back on that bus and run home to Maplewood. *Who was I kidding out here?*

But going back would just prove everyone right. That I couldn't cut it in the real world. I didn't want to spend the rest of my life winning chili cookoffs and baking pot pies for the county fair. I wanted more for myself. So I needed to suck it up, hit the pavement, and find a job.

My dream was to become a chef, but with no experience, I'd have to apply as a server first to get my foot in the door. I had waited on plenty of tables back home and my summer in Italy had taught me everything I knew about wine. So I grabbed a stack of my resumes, thin as they were, and made a bee line for the door before I talked myself out of it for real.

It took me forever to hail a cab until I realized I needed to actually stand in the middle of the street to flag one down. I wasn't even going to begin to figure out the subway system on my first day in the city. I gave the driver a mid-town Manhattan address—a swanky industrial restaurant that was the first to pop up on my search engine—and held on for dear life as the taxi charged through the city streets like a race car driver. It was a good thing I hadn't eaten breakfast because it would have likely been coming back up. I fought waves of nausea as he hit the gas, then slammed on the breaks, over and over again like a game of bumper cars.

It took me a minute to catch my breath and quell the dizziness once I was safely on the sidewalk. The crisp Autumn air did wonders for that. I pulled out one of my resumes and tugged hard on the heavy glass door leading into the restaurant.

Jazz music pumped through the speakers so loudly, I wondered how any of the diners could even have a conversation. The dining room was minimalistic with monochrome fixtures and black tablecloths. While the svelte model looking hostess was on the phone, eyeing me like I was a criminal, I scanned through the menu. *It was all in French.* I knew a few words here and there but not enough to understand every ingredient and item listed. That would no doubt be a problem.

The hostess hung up the phone and gave me a curt smile. "Sorry, we aren't hiring." Her gaze rested on the resume in my hand.

I hadn't even said a word yet. *Did I look that desperate?* "Oh. Well, can you please give this to your manager? In case something opens up?"

She rolled her eyes, clearly annoyed that I was still standing there. "I guess."

I tried to thank her, but she was already back on the phone. And something told me that the second I turned around my resume would be in the waste bin.

I pulled out my phone and scrolled to the next one on the

list—an Italian bistro a few blocks down. Forgoing the thrill ride of the taxi, and to save money, I chose to pound the pavement instead. My heels were only three inches, but they were cheaply made and by the third block, I could already feel a blister starting to form.

"Hi, I'm here about the server position." I exclaimed a little too eagerly.

This hostess's smile seemed a bit more genuine, but she couldn't hide the pity in her eyes as she looked my outfit up and down. "Thanks, hon, I'll make sure my manager gets your resume."

On my way back out, I couldn't help but notice the long line of gorgeous men and women seated along the banquette, waiting to be interviewed. Back home, if you were polite and eager to work, you'd get hired in a heartbeat. It seemed the expectations here had more to do with looks than anything else. Not that none of those people weren't qualified, but there wasn't a plain Jane in the entire bunch.

The next three restaurants I went into were a repeat of the last. Always a forced smile and a, "*Sure, we'll pass this along to the manager,*" even if none of them had any intention of doing so. It's likely they'd take one look at my short resume and toss it in the trash anyway.

The thing was, I knew food and wine. My summer abroad opened my eyes and my palate to a brand new world of exciting tastes and experiences. If someone would just give me a chance… I wouldn't be able to live here for very long if I didn't have a job. I may have failed in my relationship, but I refused to fail at this. Plus, my family didn't think I could cut it in the real world and I was determined to prove them wrong.

It was almost five o'clock in the evening and my feet were burning, but I still had two places left on my list. I was afraid if I waited until tomorrow, I'd lose my nerve. There was only so much rejection a girl could take.

The next place was *fancy*. While every other one I walked into today seemed to copy each other in décor and offerings, this restaurant stood out. It had an old-world vibe to it like something out of a classic Hollywood film. The furnishings were dark and warm with a cherrywood finish. Massive chandeliers, spanning six feet wide, decorated the vaulted ceilings, and the walls were painted a dark chocolate brown.

This restaurant was exquisite. The music was orchestral and just loud enough without drowning out the buzz of conversation. A warm sensation tickled my belly. There was something special about it. I couldn't put my finger on it, but despite the obvious display of wealth and luxury, I felt comfortable here.

"Welcome to *Dolce Sale*. How can I help you, *signorina?*" A middle-aged man with gray speckled hair peered over the podium at me.

I was in awe, still taking in the aromas wafting from the open kitchen—scents of truffle and red wine reducing into a glaze. "*Dolce Sale*," I repeated. "It means Sweet Salt. That's brilliant."

The man's smile widened, and his eyes lit up. "Ah, you speak Italian?"

I shook my head. "I know a few words here and there." I shouldn't have opened my mouth. I got his hopes up for nothing.

"You know the important ones," he teased. As he leaned forward to get a closer look at me, I noticed a nametag on the lapel of his suit that said Enzo.

I smiled and handed him my resume. "I'm looking for a job. I know I don't have a lot of experience but I'm a quick learner and I have a good palate." I had nothing left to lose today. Might as well go all out.

Enzo, so far the nicest person other than Piper that I had met in New York, nodded and scanned my resume with an arched brow. He stared at the one page as if the words were going to change before his eyes.

"As I said, I know it's not much, but I really want to learn and this place is...perfect," I continued.

"Your internship at *Ozi Wines*, in Italy, how did you like it?"

He was either making fun of me now, or genuinely confused as to how someone like me ended up there. I shifted back and forth on my throbbing feet, wishing I had worn flats instead.

"It was amazing. That experience taught me everything I know about wine and how it pairs with food. It made me want to become a chef." I glanced down, embarrassed that I had just bared part of my soul to this man I'd known for about fifteen minutes.

Enzo handed me back the resume. "You start tomorrow. Be here at 4 PM sharp to fill out paperwork. Wear black pants and black shoes. Make sure they're slip resistant. We'll provide the shirt and apron. Ozi will be pleased to hear we have given a job to one of his former interns."

I nearly fell over from shock. What were the odds? I had never met Ozi, but his contributions to the culinary world were legendary. His wines were world renowned and his restaurants were award winning. Not to mention he was also gorgeous. He was frequently photographed in those fancy society magazines, usually with a different woman on his arm every time. Not that I was paying too close attention. After what Alex put me through, the last thing I needed was to fall for another man with a wandering eye. My only focus now was my career. Love just wasn't in the cards for me.

"I'm hired? Thank you. You won't regret this. I promise."

Enzo gave me a wink. "See you tomorrow, Raven."

The pain in my heels seemed to melt away as I floated out the doors of *Dolce Sale*. Who would have thought that a summer internship five years ago would help me get a job now? Only one day in New York City and I was starting to think I made the right decision to move here after all.

Two

Ozi

"Enzo. Let the staff know I'm throwing another party tomorrow night. Double their pay." I leaned my head back and closed my eyes, waiting for his response as the skinny blonde I'd picked up this morning at the gym slid her lips up and down my dick. What was her name again? Ericka? Erin? I didn't really give a shit. They were all starting to look the same from this angle anyway.

"*Si, Signore.* I'll get everyone on board," Enzo answered back.

I clicked off the phone without another word and grabbed a fist full of blond hair. "That's it. Just like that. Don't stop."

She moaned in delight and sucked harder. They always did. All the blood in my body surged as I throbbed inside her mouth. It didn't take much to get me off these days. Partly because I was so bored and partly because I couldn't wait to get them out of my sight.

The curve of her back would do. The tip of my dick swelled, tingling as all of the blood rushed forward. I pulled out right as I was about to hit my peak and yanked her head forward. I exploded onto her lily-white back, rubbing myself back and forth as I dripped all over her.

"*Fuck*," I yelled.

She giggled and squirmed. "I would have swallowed, you know?"

Of course she would have. She took one look at my thirty-thou-sand-dollar watch and decided she would do just about anything. "Tasting me is a privilege. One you haven't yet earned." And one she wouldn't get a chance to.

I wanted her out of here so bad, I didn't bother to take the time to fetch a towel from the bathroom and instead used my shirt to clean off her back. As she got dressed, she eyed me like I was her prey. Little did she know.

"When can I see you again?" she whined.

I gave her a wink and flashed her my sexiest grin. "I'll call you, *bella*." She ate it up like candy. That Sicilian charm, the accent, it worked every time. I walked her to the door and did my best to avoid her lips, instead offering her my cheek.

She almost looked offended for a second, but another wink and she was back to having stars in her eyes. "You'll call me, right?"

"*Si. Ciao, bella.*"

I shut the door before she could utter another word. Did she sound that annoying at the gym? I wasn't trying to be an asshole and I was always respectful to their faces, but no matter how nice they were, I had no desire to get to know any of them.

Once I was sure she was gone, I exited the guest cottage and trekked back to the main house. I tugged at the collar of my shirt. Coming always made thirsty. It made me crave blood. Drinking blood was an enhanced kind of pleasure. More intimate. But the world was a different place now. I couldn't just go around drinking from the vein. Not unless I finished the job. I was a monster in many ways, but I wasn't a murderer. Not anymore.

I jogged down to the cellar and quickly emptied a blood bag into a crystal goblet. The taste of the room temperature blood had been hard to get used to. There was something so informal and empty about drinking it that way. Nothing compared to the taste of flesh, the warm blood pumping from the vein into my mouth. The scent of fear and excitement as they would writhe underneath me. They enjoyed it too once they got past the initial bite. The penetration, the exchange of blood and sex, it was the greatest pleasure on earth. But I didn't really enjoy either these days. The parties were just another distraction. A way to make the nights go by faster in an endless eternity of existence.

After a quick change of clothes, I headed up to the landing pad on my roof. The helicopter was already geared up for my trip into the city. My penthouse residence in Manhattan was the best place to entertain. And it was close to my restaurant, *Dolce Sale*, so the staff could be at my place to set up within thirty minutes. My parties always started late and continued through the night on most occasions. Last week, I'd found myself in an orgy with two supermodels and a ballet dancer. And it hadn't even been my idea. Most women were chomping at the bit to get a piece of me and I was happy to oblige. As long as they didn't want anything more.

A real relationship with a woman was not an option. The magnitude of what I was could never be comprehended by a human. I learned that lesson a long time ago. They might fantasize about it through books and movies, but the reality of a vampire in the flesh was too much for them to handle.

In just thirty minutes, we arrived at JFK airport and I climbed into the sleek black town car that was waiting for me in front. I gazed out the tinted windows as we pushed through the traffic. I loved this city at night. All the buildings lit up like stars. I sometimes wondered about the people behind those windows. I imagined them falling in love and fucking and drunk off each other. I imagined all the sinful pleasures they were enjoying and hated them for it because it was all still new and exciting to them. I envied them and their naked, quivering bodies. And I hated their humanity.

My phone beeped and a text message from my assistant, Charlie, came through.

> *Everything is set up as you like it. And there's a little gift waiting for you.*

A smile curved on my lips. Charlie was a good man. He knew what I liked and never failed to deliver.

The town car pulled up to my building and I was quickly greeted by the doorman. He grabbed my bags and followed me inside to the elevator. I swiped my card key before the elevator started climbing. I had the entire thirtieth floor and only few people had access—Enzo, Charlie, and myself. The doorman dropped my bags inside and gave me a nod as I slipped a hundred-dollar bill into his gloved hand.

I let out a deep breath. The views from up here got to me every time. The floor to ceiling windows led out to a terrace that was the size of a small football field. I could see the whole city from up here. But the view standing in front of it got me even harder.

"Welcome home, Mr. Fabiano. I've been waiting for you," the half-naked brunette cooed.

Her wavy hair stopped just short of her white breasts, exposing her taut nipples. Her stomach was flat and smooth, her hips barely holding onto her black lace panties. She leaned against the glass, parting her garter-clad thighs just enough to reveal the slit down the middle of her panties. Charlie knew me too well. She even had on fishnet stockings and five-inch black pumps. *Fuck, this was going to be fun.*

Her eyes called to me, begging me to devour her. I undressed slowly as I walked toward her, my dick fully erect. "*Ciao, bella.*"

I caught her scent before I reached her—blood mixed with cheap perfume. I could hear her heart race. She licked her lips and traced her fingers around her nipples, goading me. In one swift move, I flipped her around, pressing her tits up against the glass, and slipped my fingers between her thighs. *Damn, she was so wet.* The window fogged from her heavy breath. I reached around for her breasts and squeezed. The raspy moan that escaped from her lips sent me into a frenzy.

It was in these moments of raw desire that I forgot how miserable I was. She backed her hips into me, urging me. *"I need it, please."*

I slid my finger down the string between her ass and moved it to the side. "Bend over," I whispered into her ear. Her body shuddered as she leaned over the chair next to us. Hunger and desire took over. I pushed inside. She was so warm and wet. I almost came right then.

I used her hips to anchor me as I slid in and out, faster, and harder with each thrust. She cried out, bracing herself on the arms of the chair. Her ass bounced up and down, sending shivers up my shaft. The tip of my dick tingled as the blood rushed through, swelling, ready to burst. I couldn't hold it in much longer. Vampire senses heightened everything. The slightest touch could send me into an orgasm. This chick was saying all the right things and moaning at all the right times. *"Harder,"* she pleaded.

And I lost it. I pounded into her, my fingers digging into her hips so deep it left red marks on her white skin. "Yeah, there we go," I muttered. The tingling intensified and I squeezed into her, crying out with each ripple of pleasure.

She grunted and dragged her nails across the velvet chair, writhing and rising her hips toward me. *"Yes."* I grinded into her as I came. *Fuck, she was good.*

I ran my fingers down her spine and then pulled out slow. The brunette giggled as she reached for her coat, wasting no time to get out of there. "We should do that again sometime."

She was good, but not that good. Yet I always placated them at the end. I laid back on my couch, still naked, and let out an exasperated sigh. "Charlie will call you when I'm back in town, *bella*. Now if you don't mind, I need to get some sleep. I have a long day tomorrow," I lied.

Vampires didn't sleep. But if she stayed any longer, I was going to want to feed on her. After sex, the thirst for blood was stronger. And if I drank from her, I'd have to either kill her or turn her. I couldn't let a human run around knowing our secrets. Knowing we existed. There was no telling what would happen if the world were to find out that vampires were real.

She didn't bat an eyelash, as if she were used to these sorts of arrangements. She got off, got me off, and Charlie would make sure she was taken care of in other ways. Maybe she needed a favor or an introduction that could help her career. Either way, we were using each other. That's how it always was.

Without bothering to dress, I poured myself a glass of bourbon and gazed out the window. Alone at last and that's how I preferred it. It was the only way I could ensure that no one got too attached. Myself included. Immortality had its benefits. Emotional connection was not one of them. There was a time when connection was all I wanted. Someone to cling to in the eternal darkness. I thought I'd found her. The perfect mate. I still remember the fear in her once loving eyes as I fed her my blood. The horror on her face as she realized her human body was dying. Then the rage that erupted in her as she took on her new vampire form. The love was gone—snuffed out with her humanity. I was alone again. And so I have stayed.

Three

Raven

THERE WAS SOMETHING SENSUAL ABOUT THE WAY CHANDELIER light bounced off wine glasses, casting an intricate pattern across the table. The way it highlighted yet masked the intimate smiles and longing glances between lovers. The shared hunger in their eyes and bellies, their appetites wet as delectable dishes were placed before them. I loved the way food could make you feel things. It could sweep you away and transport you to exotic places. Make you laugh. Make you want to rip your clothes off. And it could even make you cry.

The first time I made Alex a chocolate souffle, he didn't let me leave the bedroom for two days. That's when I realized the power of food. And the appeal of a new relationship. The passion and luster quickly faded, but my desire to become a chef grew every day. Food gives you the power to create memories. To make people's fantasies come to life. To let them taste their dreams, if only for a night.

For now, I would have to settle for serving them beautiful plates and living vicariously through their faces. The not so subtle expressions of joy and awe as the sauces swirled against their tongues, morsels of tender meat chewed slow and savored, and then finished with sips of wine bursting in decadent flavors across their lips.

"*Hello*, Raven? Are you listening?" The cute perky blonde server waved a wine glass in front of my face.

"Uh, yeah. Sorry, Tori. I'm just taking it all in." Well, that wasn't going to make a great first impression.

She looked at me like I had two heads. "There's a lot to learn here, country girl. If you can't handle it, let me know now so I don't waste my time."

Country girl? "No, I'm good. I promise. Please, continue." Ever since I was a kid, my mind would wander off, daydreaming about this or that. It took a lot of focus to stay present.

I scurried after Tori throughout the restaurant as she rambled on about the menu, employee gossip, and which guests were the most important. She offered suggestions on the best ways to deal with the kitchen and showed me how to make a tableside Caesar salad. She showed me where the linens were, how to avoid locking myself in the walk-in fridge, and the *Dolce Sale* way to approach a table—which was by greeting them in Italian.

"*Buonasera.* Good evening. Welcome to *Dolce Sale*, can I start you both off with a couple of drinks? I'd highly recommend trying one of our famous Bloody Manhattans," Tori chirped. She was good at this. The couple didn't even hesitate and agreed to order whatever she told them to.

I checked the cocktail menu for reference. Bloody Manhattan—bourbon and red wine mixed with simple syrup and garnished with a black Italian cherry. Sounded fancy. It was shaken and then poured over ice into a martini glass. The handsome bartender—Max—poured some into a shot glass and offered it to me. "You gotta know what it tastes like if you're gonna sell it."

I took a small sip so as not to look like I enjoyed drinking on the job. "Delicious."

Max grinned. "It's our most popular drink. Made with top shelf bourbon, they go for twenty bucks a piece."

It made sense that Tori was pushing them on almost every table. At least on the ones who weren't already starting out with hundred-dollar bottles of wine. Everything was expensive here and the clientele proved it. While I didn't recognize all the important faces, Tori made sure to point out who was who. Everyone from supermodels, movie stars, business tycoons, to tech magnates and even politicians ate here.

The tables filled up fast and by eight PM, there wasn't an empty one in the whole place. The bar was so packed, I could barely see Max through the crowd. It made me nervous. The way Tori navigated through her section like she was throwing a party in her home, it was intimidating. Small talk didn't flow as easily for me. Back in Maplewood, I knew everyone, so there was none of that awkward ice breaking happening. And the expectations weren't exactly five star.

"Keep up, country girl. I need you to run that plate to table five and get the drink order at table three. I don't have my normal food runner tonight because of you so you better not put us in the weeds," Tori yelled as she sprinted to table six with a charcuterie platter in one hand and a plate of truffle gnocchi in the other.

I suddenly felt like I was in one of those dreams where I was naked in a room full of people. I stared down at the perfect chocolate souffle I was holding and was tempted to just chuck it and run. *Get a hold of yourself, Raven.*

I gathered myself and found table five. I set the plate down with two dessert spoons and hurried over to table three. The rowdy group of guys barely noticed me over their hollering and fist bumping. In their three-piece suits and pearly white teeth, they looked like they had walked straight off the runway. If they were this attractive in person, I could only imagine what their social media profiles looked like. We just didn't have people who looked like that in Maplewood.

"Buonasera," I said. They didn't even make eye contact. All four of them carried on with their obnoxious antics as if I weren't even there. I leaned over the table. *"Helloo.* Anyone thirsty?" I may be out of my league tonight, but I wasn't going to let them just dismiss me like I was less than.

The blond one glanced up and wrinkled his nose at me. "Seriously?"

"Just bring us the usual, darlin,'" another one with jet-black hair chimed in.

I was going to scream. "Mmm-k. Great. I'll get right on that." *What am I psychic?*

They had already forgotten about me as I stormed my way through the crowd in search of Tori. She was kneeling down next to a table full of more designer clad perfect looking people, giggling and nodding like she was their lap dog.

I leaned down and whispered in her ear while still keeping a fake smile plastered to my face, "You could have told me that table three were a bunch of asshole regulars."

If I'd offended her, she didn't show it one bit. "Excuse me, I'll be right back with your entrée's." She spun on her heel and grabbed my arm hard, dragging me away toward the bar.

"How dare you approach me like that at a table," she snapped through gritted teeth.

"You should have told about table three," I bit back.

Tori cocked her head to the side to get a better look through the dining room and let out a deep sigh of annoyance. "Oh, it's *them.* I didn't realize they were here. Still, that's no reason for you to throw a tantrum at me. You need to grow a thicker skin if you're going to make it in this business."

I wasn't trying to *make it* as a server. Someday I'd be in the kitchen, far away from the rude antics of vapid rich boys. But I did feel a little bad for taking it out on Tori. "Sorry. I thought…never mind. Who are they?"

"Friends of the owner. I don't think they are as tight with Ozi as they think they are, but they still come in here every weekend acting as if they own the place too. Look, don't worry about them. I'll get their drinks. Can you go in the back and check on the food for table six? They ordered their steaks well done but are bitching that it's taking longer than five minutes to cook them. Fucking people." She was already bee-lining over to Max before I could respond.

The rest of the night was more of the same. Every time a couple or group would pay and leave, another would be sat in their place. It was like a revolving door. There was a line out the front, at least twenty people waiting around the maître de podium, and not a single empty seat at the bar and its surrounding bar tables. And it was only 8 PM. We had at least two more hours of this. My feet burned and I didn't need to look in a mirror to know that I'd sweated off half of my makeup. I didn't know how this night could get any worse.

∞

It was almost eleven PM before the last couple finally left. Max set a glass of French Bordeaux in front of me while Tori organized her receipts for the night. "So how was your first night, country girl?" *Ugh thanks, Tori, now everyone was calling me that.*

"It was fine," I replied. Actually it was one of the most exhausting and frustrating nights of my life.

Tori handed me a twenty-dollar bill. "Thanks for your help tonight."

"Oh, I can't take that. I'm in training." The last thing I wanted was for her to bitch about how she had to tip me too.

"Whatever, just take it. Aside from a couple major screwups, you did manage to get a souffle out without dropping it." She winked at Max who put his head down as he laughed.

I could feel my cheeks burning. It was bad enough that she gave me bad directions all night, but now she was making fun of me in front of the other staff members. I couldn't wait to get home and crawl into bed. I downed the rest of my wine, shoved the twenty into my apron pocket and slid off the bar stool.

"Where do you think you're going, country girl?" Tori cooed.

The muscles between my shoulder blades tightened. "Home. Unless there's anything else you need me to do?"

Tori and Max burst out laughing just as three other servers sauntered up. Max rested his elbows on the bar, gazing back at me with half amusement, half pity. "Hate to break this to ya, Raven, but you aren't going home for a while."

Before I could ask him what he was talking about, Enzo appeared. "Okay, *bambinos*, you know the deal. The cars will be out front in five minutes. Freshen up and look presentable. I don't want to keep Ozi waiting."

What in the world? I must have looked like a deer caught in the headlights because Enzo's eyes widened at the sight of me. "Oh, Raven, I'm so sorry I forgot to tell you. Ozi is throwing one of his famous parties tonight. He doesn't like to hire outside caterers. It's very simple, just passing out drinks and small bites. You'll get paid double your hourly wage."

I was going to be sick. The newly formed blisters on my feet were making it hard to stand, let alone work an entirely other shift. But with the double pay, I could get ahead on some of my bills. Besides, if I said no, how would that make me look? I was the new girl and half the staff already thought I was a joke. If I crawled home while they all went and worked another shift, I'd never earn their respect. Not to mention the owner would wonder why his most recent new hire was already slacking off.

"Of course, Enzo. I'll just go freshen up." I forced a smile and tried not to look like I was going to pass out.

"*Grazie*, Raven! I know you're tired, but I appreciate you being a team player."

As I sulked into the ladies room, I couldn't help but overhear Tori giving the rest of the staff a play by play of how slow and incompetent I was. *Ugh this was going to be a long night.*

Four

Ozi

I SMEARED THE STEAM OFF THE MIRROR WITH A FUZZY TOWEL, admiring my own reflection. While guiding a thick glob of hair gel through my black waves, I slicked them back off my tanned forehead. I dabbed my favorite cologne along my neck—a mix of spice and sandalwood, rubbing some into my chest as well. It was no wonder mortal women couldn't keep their hands off me. Immortality had made me into a god. Made my body strong and chiseled, my features striking with piercing brown eyes and long black lashes. It was almost unfair to human men.

The vein in my neck throbbed. My pectoral muscles twitched and constricted. I needed to drink before I went downstairs into a room full of delicious snacks. And I wasn't referring to the food. I reached for the blood bag I'd retrieved from the cellar earlier and tore into it. The room temperature blood oozed down my throat like molasses, except it tasted like a bottle of wine that had been left open for too long—sour like vinegar. I got it down as fast as I could, chasing it with a shot of bourbon.

Curling my upper lip, I watched the two sharp fangs retreat slightly into my gums, making their points even with the rest of my teeth. While they weren't noticeable, there were these tiny little nerve endings that sent titillating sensations throughout my body, similar to an orgasm. They were extremely sensitive and coupled with the ecstasy and taste of fresh blood, it was a big part of the exquisite gratification.

And when I'm coming and feeding at the same time...*fuck* it was the best feeling in the world. I used to think love was until it weakened me. Or rather, the lack of reciprocated love had. Too much loss and pain could do that to you. Make you bitter and cold. I had never loved anyone the way I loved Camille. And I never wanted to again.

So the parties were for my amusement. For my entertainment. When the reality of my existence was too much to bear, the exhilaration and beauty of painted faces, glittered skin, and intoxication was what I craved. Sometimes more than anything else. But blood was better than love. Blood was bonding. As was death and it did not taste the same anymore. Neither did the booze or the women. All of it had lost its shine and luster. But I was afraid of who I'd be if I stopped any of it.

I headed downstairs to see my penthouse springing to life. The scent of garlic and puff pastry wafted through the air. Staff buzzed around setting up food stations and opening bottles of wine. The guests would be arriving soon. And to their delight, I had pulled out all the stops. I needed extra distractions tonight to keep me from remembering the anniversary of her human death. I couldn't let myself go down memory road again. It would only lead to destruction—of myself and those around me. It was one hundred years ago, but it felt like yesterday. One of the downfalls of living forever.

Enzo arrived with the *Dolce Sale* staff and sent them directly into the kitchen to load up their trays with flutes of sparkling wine and hors d'oeuvres. I didn't bother to greet them. I wasn't in the mood for pleasantries and small talk just yet. Instead, I walked to the glass ledge of the terrace and took in the view of the city and wondered how many women would try to end up in my bed tonight. Maybe I'd let them all have a piece of me. *Would that be enough to help me forget?*

Within minutes, the first of my guests started to arrive and I headed over to them, mustering up all my charm and sex appeal on the way. A lanky blonde, accompanied by some greasy financial guy, strutted up, meeting me half way. She blew air kisses and fluttered her eyelashes. "Ozi, what a fabulous home you have."

I flashed her a toothy grin. "It's more of a lion's den than a home, *bella*," I teased. "But I'll take it. Go see Max over there at the bar. Tell him I sent you." I winked and I swear her nipples hardened instantly. *Fuck, this was so easy.*

Raven

The string quartet had set up on the terrace and had begun playing. They were the best in the industry, I was told. While their violins and flutes blasted out, making top forty hits sound like classical masterpieces, the city lights sprawled out behind them. It was like a page out of a magazine or a dark fairytale. The penthouse was enormous, it was hard to believe the owner lived here all by himself.

I wound in and out of the glittering crowd in awe. Every face I passed looked like it had been photoshopped. If only my friends in Maplewood could see this, they wouldn't believe it. I barely did. These people didn't exist in real life. But here they were, in the flesh. They were gorgeous and they knew it. I weaved in and out unnoticed. They took the flutes of sparkling *Ozi* wine without so much as a nod or facial acknowledgement. They were used to pretending staff were invisible. I actually liked it. It kept me from having to make idle small talk with strangers.

Once everyone had a glass and a decent helping of small bites, I and another server stood alert by the floor to ceiling French doors that separated the living room from the terrace, now wide open for foot traffic to pass through. I breathed in the crisp fresh air, listened to the sounds of car horns and sirens erupting from down below. We were thirty floors up and this view of the city was even more spectacular than the one from my apartment. It was breathtaking.

I looked across the terrace at all of the too perfect faces and froze. The most beautiful man I'd ever seen in my life was just a few feet away. He laughed and leaned into a group of pretty blondes. He was tall and muscular with black hair and brown eyes. His black suit was tailored to him like a glove and looked expensive. *Oh shit.* It was him. Ozi. The owner of *Dolce Sale*...my new boss. His pictures did not do him justice.

I willed myself to look away. I didn't want Enzo or any of the other staff members to catch me gawking at him. I tried to focus on the skyline but my gaze kept wandering back over to this gorgeous specimen of a man. Men didn't look like that in Maplewood. Sure we had our share of handsome boys next door, but not like this. This man could make women do whatever he wanted. I was getting dizzy just thinking about it. *Why was he making me feel tingly all over?* I didn't come here for that.

It had only been a year since Alex broke my trust and my heart. I didn't know if I'd ever be ready to love again, let alone even date. I was so empty inside... What would I even have to offer? The betrayal left a wound so deep, I wasn't sure the bleeding had ever stopped. But *damn*, Ozi was sexy. The way he licked his full lips with each sip of his whiskey, it was giving me all kinds of wicked thoughts. Like what else that tongue of his could do.

I spun around toward the bar and cornered Max.

"Do you have the next round of drinks? I'm getting bored out here." Truth was I needed something to drag my attention away from our hot boss.

"Okay, girl. I see you." He winked as he handed me a tray of old fashions. Oh dear god. *Did he see me salivating over Ozi?* I was mortified. I stared down at my tray and wished I could disappear into one of the glasses. The whiskey was a creamy caramel color, offset by the dark juicy black Italian cherry and bright orange peel.

I immediately started drifting in and out of the crowd, passing out drinks like they were candy. The guests didn't hesitate, lapping them up like water. I kept my back strategically turned away from Ozi. The last thing I needed was to get flustered and drop this entire tray of drinks on some spoiled socialite. I wasn't a clumsy person but Ozi made me nervous. There was something about the way he leaned into the woman he was chatting with. The way his lips hovered over her ear as she threw her head back in laughter at whatever charming thing he had said. I bet he smelled good too. *Stop it, Raven. Get your head in the game.*

The music seemed to get louder with each strum of the violin and it reverberated through me, enchanting me like a dream. What time was it? It had to be close to midnight. I stifled a yawn and went back toward the bar to fill up my tray.

"Raven, there you are. Don't wander too far, I'd like you to meet the owner later," Enzo said. "If I can ever pull him away from that blonde over there."

I followed the direction of his gaze and felt all the blood rush to my cheeks. I had completely forgotten that I'd have to meet him. Of course he would want to meet his new employee. How was I going to keep my cool when just one look at him sent my pulse racing? *Shit.*

Within an hour, the terrace was filled with beautiful people in designer clothes, gathering to partake in my free food and booze. As vapid and dull as most of these people were, they temporarily filled a void that would allow me to pretend I was like them for the night.

"Mr. Fabiano, is everything to your liking?" Like a ghost, Enzo appeared out of nowhere. If I didn't know for certain that he was human, I would have sworn he was a vampire.

"*Si, Grazie*, Enzo. You have outdone yourself as usual." Enzo had been with me for thirty years. He knew me better than anyone.

"We have a new girl here tonight. She interned at *Ozi Wines* in Italy. She is a little out of her element, but catches on quick," Enzo said.

I glanced around the terrace and spotted her. It was easy to do because I made a point to know every single person who worked for me. I had a file on each of them. The new girl's back was turned but I could see she was petite with a perfectly tight ass and long black hair that was swept up into a ponytail. "You'll introduce me to her later, no? What's her name?"

Enzo smiled wearily. No matter how old or tired he got, he refused to let me turn him. He said it was against his beliefs. Stubborn old bastard. Though, he never judged me for what I was. "Her name is Raven. She's inexperienced, but she knows her wines and has an excellent palate."

"Good. *Belissimo*. I trust your judgement, Enzo. That's why you handle all the hiring. You must see something special in her." Enzo had a soft spot for wayward souls. Sometimes it worked out and they went on to have great careers in the food and beverage industry. And on the rare occasion they turned out to be psycho, he was the one that dealt with the restraining orders. Hopefully, this Raven girl wouldn't turn out to be the latter.

Enzo sighed. He looked to Raven, who still had her back turned, and then to me. "Promise me you won't try to sleep with this one. She is very naïve and I think you would ruin her. She has dreams of becoming a chef. I wouldn't want her getting distracted by your dick."

A tiny spurt of wine spewed out of my mouth as I burst out laughing. Enzo had never been the shy type, but that was the bluntest thing he'd ever said to me. I liked it. "You make me out to be some kind of sex monster," I joked. "Relax, the days of me screwing the staff are long over. That was when, the eighties? In Paris? You must really like this one, old man."

Enzo's cheeks reddened as he smiled sheepishly. "I do. She is different. This city will eat her alive if we don't watch out for her."

It almost seemed like he was getting fatherly protective over her. Enzo never married and never had children, so maybe this was his way of adopting. I just hoped she didn't disappoint him. "Listen, I'll meet you at the bar in a few so you can introduce me to your new *protégé*. I need to make a couple more laps around the terrace before these assholes get too drunk to remember I was a gracious host."

As I continued to make my rounds through the crowd, my eye kept getting drawn back toward the new hire. I couldn't explain it but I needed her to turn around. I wanted to see her face. The way she moved gracefully across the terrace drew me in. The curves of her hips and ass, bouncing as she walked, stirred something primal in me, reminding me I was a predator.

I would look but not touch as I'd promised Enzo, but I needed to see more of her. I could sift out the scent of her blood amidst all of these people and it was intoxicating. Her blood was pure, sweet, but filled with nervous energy and a hint of mystery. And something else. Something familiar.

My mouth watered the more I thought about her. I unbuttoned the top of my shirt as visions of tasting her began to choke me. I'd had plenty of blood before the party started but this woman's scent was making my glands salivate. Just her sheer presence made me thirsty. Coupled with all the noise from a thousand conversations blaring in my ears—conversations I could hear from a mile away thanks to heightened vampire senses—it was dizzying.

I darted in and out of the crowd, trying to make my way back into the main penthouse. If I were going to meet this woman, I would need more blood, or risk coming unglued in front of all these people. I'd always prided myself on being discreet and I'd had hundreds of years of practice, but her blood was getting to me as if I hadn't fed in days.

I was almost to the living room when one of my business associates cut me off. "Ozi, we need to talk. I found some weird shit going on with one of our accounts."

Cassius—a giant behemoth of a man covered in tattoos with long dirty blond hair that he swept back into a ponytail—towered over me. He was my business partner and an old friend, but he had terrible timing.

"Cassius. Hello to you too. Can it wait? I need to pop into the storage room before I explode." I needed to get at least one shot of blood in me before I unraveled.

He looked me over, his gaze settling on the throbbing vein in my neck and nodded in understanding. "Get your shit right, Ozi. I'll find you later."

I pushed past him and practically sprinted into the kitchen. I kept an emergency stash in the walk-in pantry and quickened my pace to get to it. My body was trembling and I couldn't get in there fast enough. I quickly shut the door behind me and punched the code into the safe where I had hid the blood bags. I ripped into one and sucked every bit out as fast as I could. Slumping back against the wall, relief spread into my veins. My heart rate surged and then slowed back down to a normal pace. It was the blood that kept it beating. My liquid pacemaker.

Fuck me, that was close.

I wiped the sweat off my brow with a kitchen rag, straightened my collar, and went back out into the party.

"Ozi," Enzo called for me. He squeezed my elbow and guided me toward the bar. "Remember, play nice."

I was still out of sorts but my head was starting to clear. The crisp night air cooled the sweat on the back of my neck and it felt amazing. Everything was always heightened. The slightest breeze could feel like tiny fingertips stroking my face. It was as if the wind were seducing me.

As we approached the brunette, her scent nearly stopped me in my tracks. It was jarring. I could hear her heart race as Enzo spoke to her. She hesitated, then turned toward me, and it took everything in my power not to pounce.

Raven

"Raven Monroe, I'd like you to meet your new boss, the esteemed owner of *Dolce Sale*. I present to you, Ozi Fabiano."

I whipped around with my hand out ready to shake and lost my breath. *It was him.* The man I'd been ogling all night. Our eyes met and it was as if the whole room blurred around me. We stared at each other without speaking. My heart raced like a speeding train, threatening to crash and burn into a million pieces. It wasn't until Enzo dramatically cleared his throat that I was able to snap back into reality.

Ozi took my hand, but instead of shaking it, he brought it to his lips and placed the softest kiss on my skin that I had ever felt. Every nerve in my body tingled. A slight, almost unnoticeable quiver of warm breath brushed over my knuckles. "It's a pleasure, *signorina*. Welcome to the family." His voice, heavily soaked in his Italian accent, was deep and rich and melodic. And it vibrated through me like the violins.

"Thank you for this opportunity," was all I could muster. I sounded like a robot but I was on the verge of passing out. His presence was dizzying. Intoxicating. A sense of guilt washed over me. I had been lusting after him all night, but he was my boss. Off limits and a very bad idea for multiple reasons. I needed this job and I couldn't risk anything screwing it up. I also had no intention of letting my guard down around a man anytime soon. Even one that looked like him.

"I was just telling Ozi how you interned at his vineyard years ago. No one else at *Dolce Sale* has even visited. Raven, tell us what you learned there." Enzo was trying to steer the conversation into a more professional direction and I was grateful.

My mouth was so dry, I wished I could have grabbed one of the flutes of sparkling wine that whizzed by me. "It…It was one of the best times of my life. I stayed in the guest house and got to wake up in the middle of a vineyard in Tuscany every day. I picked olives and learned how to make cheese. Sometimes I wish I were still back there." I felt like I had said too much but it was true. My time on Ozi's vineyard was the last time I remembered being truly happy.

"I'm surprised we never crossed paths. I must have just missed you. I tend to spend my winters there. I find the New York winters a bit depressing. I'd love to hear more about it sometime." Ozi didn't blink or take his eyes off of me. He was one of the most present people I'd ever spoken to. Most people were often distracted or thinking about what they were going to say next. But not Ozi. He literally savored and noted every word I said. He was completely in tune to me and seemed to forget that Enzo was still standing there.

"I would like that," I murmured. Oh dear god, he still had the tips of my fingers in his hand.

"All right, we kept you long enough, Raven. Max is making drinks faster than everyone can get them out. I swear, he's too efficient for his own good sometimes." Enzo chuckled and made a shooing motion with his hands.

I nodded and I swear I almost curtsied toward Ozi. *What in the hell was wrong with me?*

"It was nice to meet you, sir. I—"

"Please, call me Ozi," he interjected.

I pulled my hand away under Enzo's curious stare. "I better get back."

"Of course. I will see you again." Ozi didn't break eye contact with me until I turned around. I could have held his gaze all night long.

I rushed back over to Max, my face flushed and my lower back pooling in sweat. "Sorry about that. Enzo wanted me to meet Ozi."

Max arched an eyebrow at me. "Whatever you say, country girl. Now please get these drinks out of my sight. I can't even look at them anymore. Who fucking drinks white zin anyways?" He looked like he was actually disgusted. I couldn't help but giggle at him. And it was enough to snap me out of my stupor.

I didn't run into Ozi again for the rest of the night, but I could still feel his gaze on me from across the terrace. I stole a peek every twenty minutes or so and I was right. He was watching me. It was probably just because I was the new girl and he wanted to make sure I didn't screw up his party. At least that's what I kept telling myself.

We finished cleaning up around two AM and I made it home by three. As exhausted as I was, I laid in bed wide awake. I couldn't stop thinking about him. *I will see you again.* I couldn't get the sound of his voice out of my head. This was not good. I came to New York to become a chef, not to have fantasies about my hot new boss. So how was I going to work for a man that made me want to rip his clothes off?

Five

Ozi

CASSIUS WAS SEATED IN THE LIVING ROOM. "WHAT, NO HOT model waiting for you tonight? You must be losing your touch."

I laughed as I poured us a couple whiskeys. Cassius knew me well. We had been partners for a long time, and friends even longer. I was still reeling from Raven's presence that I hadn't even bothered to notice that the party had cleared out before I could make my move on anyone.

"Watch your tongue," I teased. "I already played twice today. Besides, we need to discuss whatever it is you're concerned about."

His smile faded. "It's about our black account. I think someone is trying to hack into it. And with Lux out of the country on one of his little artifact expeditions, that leaves just you and me to figure it out."

"I thought that account was unbreachable, Cassius. We can't afford to have any of it leak out. You have to fix this. I can't be seen anywhere near this. My presence is too public." Our black account belonged to me, Cassius, and Lux, and it contained all our hidden assets and black-market dealings. It could also point out to what we were. *Immortal.*

Cassius paced around my living room, his wolf eyes glowing gold. "I know. I'm working on it. This is why you should never have turned yourself into a public playboy. You draw too much attention to yourself. Lux and I warned you about it decades ago." While the three of us were well over a hundred years old, neither of us looked a day over thirty.

"Well, forgive me for not wanting to hide out in the wilderness like you. Or lock myself in an ivory tower as Lux has done. What's the fun in being the strongest creature in the world if you can't reap the carnal benefits?" I winked over my glass.

He huffed and slumped down onto my black leather couch. "And you, my friend, have *too* much fun. Anyhow, I've got my team on it. I'll send word to Lux when he checks in. I just have a bad feeling about this."

Cassius was always the most paranoid out of the three of us.

I wagged my finger at him. "You, *my friend*, don't have enough fun. Aren't you wolves designed to mate? When was the last time you had a woman in your bed?"

"None of your business, Ozi." His brow scrunched together as he looked away.

"Look, I trust you will get to the bottom of this. We are the Sons of the Fallen. Don't ever forget that. People don't just stumble upon us." We were an organization of only three for a reason. While there were plenty of immortals out there, most could not be trusted. Lux and Cassius had proven their loyalty to me and I to them. We got lucky in finding each other. If someone was trying to hack into our accounts, it had to be some nosy human. No other immortal would be stupid enough to cross us.

Cassius nodded and went for his coat. "I'll show myself out. I'll let you know if I find out anything substantial."

"I have total faith in you, brother," I called out as he reached the front door. "And try to have some fun for once. Life is short for them but long and boring for us."

"Yeah, yeah," Cassius muttered as he shut the door behind him.

Now that I was finally alone, I let my mind drift back to earlier. To Raven. I wanted her. I wanted to taste every part of her. She was different. But Enzo would never let me hear the end of it. Plus, I knew that the second I had her, she'd fall. She'd want more. And I wasn't sure I trusted myself not to drink from her either. I couldn't let my desire cloud my judgement.

But she was sexy as hell and her restrained demeanor, the way she was so tightly wound, suggested something wilder lurking beneath the surface. The thought of her writhing underneath me made my dick so hard, I regretted not lining up someone to fuck tonight.

It was almost four in the morning by the time I had made up my mind. I had said I'd stay away, but I had to see her face again. *Fuck Enzo.* It was my restaurant and she was my employee. I would do with her what I wanted.

I watched the sun come up while sipping a cup of black coffee then picked up my phone and dialed Enzo. "I'm not ready to leave the city. Have my usual table ready for me. I'll be there around nine PM."

"*Si, signor.* Any special requests I can have prepared for you?" Enzo sounded groggy. I must have woken him.

"Yes. Make sure Raven is my server."

Silence.

"Enzo?"

He cleared his throat. "*Si, si.* Of course, but—"

I hung up before he could finish.

❧

By the time my black stretch town car rolled up to the front of *Dolce Sale*, I was starting to regret my decision. It wasn't like me to dine alone. I had to fix that.

Charlie picked up on the first ring. "Mr. Fabiano, what can I do for you tonight?"

"I need a date, blond preferably, and I need her to be here in five minutes. The more adventurous the better." I needed a distraction and to show Enzo *and* Raven that I wasn't readily available.

"You got it, boss. I'll have her there in four." Charlie hung up before I could respond. That was what I liked about him. No casual chit-chat. No bullshit. He just got the job done.

And in three minutes, a tall voluptuous blond goddess tapped on my window. She wore a black lace mini dress with a plunging neckline, so tight it looked as if it had been painted on. Her makeup was slightly smudged around her eyes and a fresh sheen of sweat glittered across her half-exposed breasts. And I could smell the vodka in her blood.

I gave her the standard Italian greeting, a kiss on each cheek. "Looks like you've already started the party without me, *bella*. Are you hungry?" I whispered suggestively in her ear.

She licked her lips as the back of her hand grazed my crotch. "*Starving.*"

We were seated at my usual table in the back—a dark corner in which I could discreetly keep an eye on everything on the dining room floor. Before I could even fully sit down in my chair, my date's pale white hand was already traveling up my thigh.

"Easy, *bella*. That's for dessert," I cooed in her ear.

She laughed throatily. "Mmm, my favorite course." I swept a strand of her hair back so I could nibble on her ear.

"Hello—hi." Raven cleared her throat. "Can I start you two off with something to drink?"

My pulse raced. *How about your blood?* "We'll take a bottle of *sangiovese* from my label. The private reserve. How are you this evening?"

She was doing her best to not gawk at my semi-clad date. I could see the heat rushing to her cheeks, hear the racing of her heart, the throbbing in her pulse. "Wonderful, thank you for asking. I'll be right back with your thigh—I mean your wine."

I couldn't stop the grin from spreading across my face. She rushed off and almost knocked a whole tray over on her way to the wine cellar. I was getting under her skin. This was going to be fun.

Raven

Why was he here?

Yes, it was his restaurant but the other servers said he rarely came in. And why did he request me to wait on him and the half-naked bombshell? She looked like a porn star. And here I was, miss *country girl*, lusting after a man so far out of my league, I wasn't even on the correct playing field.

I found the wine he requested and almost tripped again on the way back to his table. Apparently every time I got around Ozi, I seemed to lose all motor functions. He must've thought I was the biggest klutz on the planet.

"Did you go to Italy to get the wine?" the blonde quipped, laughing at her own joke.

"Sorry, I'm new here. It took me a minute to find it." I unscrewed the cork while avoiding his stare.

Ozi gave my elbow a light squeeze. "No need to apologize, Raven. I have all the time in the world."

Our eyes locked and a tingle sparked between my legs like an electric shock. The blonde scooted closer to him and draped her arm across his back. "I think we need a few more minutes to decide on what we want to eat. Unless *he's* on the menu, of course."

Oh my god, every time this chick opened her mouth something stupid came out. Ozi shrank back a bit and forced a tight smile. Was this really his type? *The dumber, the better, I guess.*

After another three attempts to get their order, they finally decided on another bottle of wine and oysters on the half shell. I tried not to cringe every time he fed her one. It was like watching a child giggle over a piece of candy, the over-dramatic way she squealed with delight after each raw slippery oyster slid down her throat.

"How did you get so lucky to have Ozi in your section?" Tori snapped. She couldn't keep the jealousy out of her voice.

"Yeah, lucky me. They are practically having sex on the table. I feel so privileged," I snapped back. It was bad enough I had to deal with Ozi's arrogance, I didn't have it in me to deal with Tori's taunts tonight too.

She snickered and rolled her eyes as if I were the one being dramatic now. "Whatever you say, country girl."

Max flashed me a toothy grin. "Girl, ignore her. She's just threatened by you. You're young, pretty, and about to receive a big tip from the owner. Ozi always leaves at least a hundred. Even if he orders a salad."

"He better. At least for putting up with the little display he's got going on with that bimbo," I quipped.

Max laughed as he read the incoming ticket and reached for a martini shaker. "Hey, you should get drinks with us later. It's sort of an after-work ritual. It will give you a chance to get to know everyone."

The last thing I wanted was to have to divulge personal information about myself to total strangers. *What if I have too many drinks and accidentally spill my sad pathetic relationship drama?* Talk about a buzz kill. Alex always said I had *loose lips* when I was drunk. Too bad he had a loose dick when I wasn't around.

But if I closed myself off too much, I'd always be an outsider here. "Sure. That sounds like fun."

I tried to discreetly drop the check but Ozi took notice. "Raven, excellent job this evening. I believe you are fitting in here well. Thank you for your attention to detail." He gave me a wink and the blonde at his side rolled her eyes.

He was enjoying it. The way his date vied for his attention. He loved the way I floundered and flustered about in his presence. Ozi must have known the affect he had on women and he relished it. He lapped it up like a dog. His arrogance was beginning to annoy me.

"Of course, sir. Have a wonderful evening." I turned to leave but he caught me by the arm. I felt the crisp fold of a bill in my palm.

"Drinks are on me tonight, darling." His gaze flitted over my lips.

"How did you know—"

"It's tradition. The staff goes out together every Friday night. Unless, of course, you won't be joining them?" Ozi rested his hand on the blonde's leg, which delighted her as she was beginning to scowl at the lack of attention.

"It would be rude of me to turn it down. Thank you again." I shoved the bill without looking at it into my apron pocket and hastened my way back to the bar. The rest of the night was uneventful and I managed to avoid Ozi's table until they left. I gathered my things and stepped out into the chilly New York City night.

Max was out front, scrolling through his phone. "There you are. The others went on ahead. The bar's just a few blocks away." I followed him as he walked.

"Thanks for waiting for me. So what's the name of the bar?" I asked as if I knew anything about the bars in this city.

Max combed through his dark curls with his gloved fingers. "The Red Apothecary. It used to be an old pharmacy back in the day. The drinks are awesome. They've named them after old medicines and ancient remedies. And the décor is gorgeous—dark lighting, velvet drapes, very vintage chic."

"I can't wait. We only have two bars in Maplewood." There was a dirty saloon that was older than the town itself and known to get rowdy on a weeknight, and a wine bar that no one went to because the locals thought it was too bougie for them.

Max laughed and linked his arm in mine. "You're a long way from home, country girl."

As we skipped down Fifth Avenue, he couldn't have been more right. Every corner I turned reminded me of just how strange I must look to all the rest. We were almost to the entrance of the bar when I heard a low whisper against the wind. A chill traveled up my spine and I spun around. No one was there but I had the oddest feeling that someone was watching me.

Six

Ozi

THE MUSIC WAS ALWAYS TOO LOUD AT THE RED APOTHECARY. ...es were already heightened enough as it was and with this blonde nibbling on my ear, it was even harder to make out the conversation happening at the bar. Raven had just walked in with Max and I was straining to eavesdrop on them.

She hadn't noticed me yet. *But she will.* I sent the blonde off to the dancefloor with a shot of their best whiskey and fixed my gaze on Raven, willing her to turn around. And like clockwork her eyes shifted to the dark corner of the bar that I was lurking in.

The breath caught in her throat. I could tell by the way her chest rose and her lips quivered. There was so much longing in her eyes. So much hunger. I wanted to taste it. She jerked her head away, turning back toward Max and the others. I was left to admire her long dark hair, its ends nearly reaching the top of her tight ass. Watching the curve of her hips sway back and forth to the music made my dick rock hard.

Just once would be okay. *It would only be once.* I could never fuck the same woman twice anyway. Aside from the fact that they didn't respond well to being kicked out just minutes after I came all over them, I couldn't let anyone get too close. More than a one-night stand would lead to expectations and questions and wanting more. Human women always wanted more. They were never satisfied. I was insatiable as well but I could find pleasure in a different one every time.

The problem of late was that they were all starting to feel the same. There was nothing new or exciting about these women. I was just going through the motions. Getting off and sending them out. Some nights I could make myself come better. But Raven...she piqued my interest. Something told me that she would taste different. As tightly wound as she was, she'd be anything but boring.

"Hello, Ozi. It's been a long time." The sound of her voice instantly killed my erection. I turned to see another blonde who had caused me more grief than anyone I'd ever met.

"Camille...What are you doing in my city?"

She ran a long, pointy fingernail down the collar of my shirt. "*Your* city? I had forgotten what an arrogant ass you are. I have business here that doesn't concern you."

"Then why do I feel concerned? Your idea of conducting business usually leads to a trail of dead bodies and empty bank accounts." Now I was beginning to wonder if this was merely a coincidence that Camille had resurfaced just as our bank account was being hacked into.

She snatched my drink and helped herself to it. "And who's fault is that? Don't deny your part in my existence, my love. Perhaps you should have killed me instead..."

"Don't talk like that. You know that was never an option for me. Tell me why you are really here, Camille."

"I told you. I have a business opportunity that I couldn't pass up. Surely there's room for two vampires in *your* city. I promise to stay out of your way, lover." She let that last word roll off her tongue like a cat purring.

"Oh, like you stayed out of my way in Paris? Can you blame me for being alarmed?" I didn't trust her then and I don't trust her now.

"Please, Ozi, that was a hundred years ago. You always were one to hold a grudge."

"Look who's talking. You've never forgiven me for...." I couldn't even bring myself to say it out loud.

A hint of venom flashed in her eyes and dissipated as quickly as it appeared. "Nonsense. It's all in the past. I'm ready to move forward. Besides, you have your immortality and all the money in the world. Can't I just have this one thing? You owe me."

And there it was. The thing she would hang over my head for eternity and never let me forget. She would always use my guilt to get what she wanted. "Fine. But if you meddle in any of my affairs, you will regret coming here. Debt or no debt, I've worked too hard to have you come in here and fuck it all up."

She smiled but it didn't reach her eyes. "I wouldn't dream of it."

I looked away for a moment and she was gone. I scanned the bar but there was no sign of her. Camille always was a slippery one. Despite all my warnings to not show her speed in public, she defied me. It was more than just her messing with my money, it was about her potentially exposing all of us. She was unstable and reckless and she didn't care about the humans. She would rather have her fun and then bury all the witnesses.

I searched the room for my date and spotted her making out with an equally attractive woman. She caught my eye and curled her finger at me, beckoning me to join them. Two were always more fun than one, but Raven was still at the bar, avoiding eye contact with me, and I was angry at myself for caring. This whole night was pissing me off. *Fuck it. I'm just going to go over there and talk to her.* I downed the rest of my drink and parted my way through the crowd.

As I got closer to the bar, Raven whipped out her phone and held it to her ear. Her face fell and her eyes welled up. A group of drunk women intercepted me, groping my ass, and grinding up against me. They blocked my way but I pushed past them without using my full strength. Didn't want to risk knocking any of them over. I kept my eyes on Raven. She whispered something to Max before grabbing her coat and bolting out the front door.

Max waved at me as I approached. "Hey, boss. Can I buy you a drink?"

"I'll buy *you* stock in this bar if you tell me why Raven ran off like that." I didn't care if my question sparked rumors. It had been a shitty night and the only woman I wanted to fuck was the only woman who seemed to want nothing to do with me.

Max looked around to make sure no one was listening and then leaned in close. "I don't think anyone died or anything, but something bad happened. All she said to me was that she just got the worst news of her life."

I nodded, pulled out my phone, and sent a quick text. I patted Max on the back. "Thank you. You now own ten shares in the Red Apothecary."

The look on his face was priceless. I stormed out before he could respond, leaving my date and the chilling feeling of dread behind me.

This was the first night in a hundred years that I had no interest in meaningless sex. Camille showing up in the city had put me in a foul mood and the way Raven left the bar without me getting a chance to speak with her made me even more annoyed.

I pulled out my phone as the elevator doors opened to my floor and dialed Cassius.

"What's up, Ozi?" His voice was strained and it sounded like he hadn't been sleeping.

"Camille is in town. I need you to keep an eye on her."

"Do you think she has anything to do with our account being hacked?"

"I'm not sure, but I wouldn't put it past her. Just be on alert."

I clicked "end call" before he could start asking me about my feelings. Cassius was a sensitive brute and I was not in the mood to be probed about the very old and very over relationship with my ex-girlfriend.

I contemplated calling Raven to see if she was all right but stopped myself. Why did I care? Nothing good ever came from caring for humans. They didn't have the mental or emotional capacity to love the way us immortals did. That was why we never showed them what we really were. They scared too easily and did not understand anything that was different from them. They'd judge us and then want to study us like lab rats.

Why would Raven be any different than Camille? I'd trusted *her* once. Gave her my heart and shared with her my secrets…and she rejected me. She wouldn't ever forgive me for turning her and I wouldn't ever forgive myself for dropping my guard. For letting her glimpse the darkest parts of me only for her to cast me aside. The pleasures of the flesh were all I'd allow myself to feel now. But not tonight. Tonight I just wanted to wallow in my self-pity.

Seven

Raven

I WAS GOING TO BE SICK. NOT BECAUSE THE TAXI DRIVER WAS zipping in and out of traffic like we were in the middle of a car chase, which didn't help, but because of the voicemail. I should have waited till I got home to listen to it. But as soon as I saw the caller ID, I couldn't stop myself.

They were getting married.

Alex and Meadow. It was bad enough that he had cheated on me with her, but now they were getting married, and he would be in my family forever. What disgusted me even more was I had to hear it from him. Meadow—my own sister—didn't even bother to tell me that she was marrying the boyfriend she stole from me. How could my parents be okay with this? How could anyone? But she was always their favorite so it was no surprise when they sided with her and blamed me for not being a good enough partner to him.

But marriage?

It was amazing how one phone call could change everything. Spin the world upside down till nothing could ever be the same again, even when the room stopped spinning. I knew in my bones that I would never be going back to Maplewood. It was no longer my home. I bit my lip hard to stop the tears from falling. I refused to lose it in the back of a New York City cab.

There was nothing left to do but cry myself to sleep. I turned the key into an empty apartment and poured myself a glass of wine. The city lights reflecting on the windows did nothing to ease my pain, as beautiful and ethereal as they were. The love of my life had officially moved on and I was in a strange city, nowhere closer to my dreams than I was the day I left.

I finished my wine and crawled into bed, thankful that I had tomorrow off so I could sleep in. In fact, I wasn't sure I was even going to get out of bed at all.

∿

The loud banging on my door jarred me awake. Was Piper back early? Did she forget her key? There was no one else I could think of that would come over unannounced. I dragged myself out of bed and pulled on my fluffy white robe.

"Coming," I yelled. My head was pounding from crying and too much wine. I glanced through the peephole and everything about last night came flooding back. "Shit," I cursed under my breath.

I opened the door and there was Max, bright eyed and holding two cups of steaming hot coffee. "You forgot, didn't you?"

After three fruity cocktails at Red Apothecary last night, I had agreed to hang out with Max all day and have him show me around the city. "I did. I'm so sorry. It was a rough night."

Max shoved one of the coffees in my hand and let himself in. "No worries. I'll wait while you get ready."

"Uh, Max, I'm not feeling up to it today. I'm still processing some news I got last night." What was it going to take to get rid of him?

Max waltzed over to the window and looked out. "This view is on point. Look, Raven, whatever it is that's got you so upset, you can't just sit here all day by yourself and wallow in it. You gotta get out and get some fresh air. And if you want to talk about it, I'm a good listener."

I was starting to get the feeling that he was being a little too pushy. "Max…you're sweet and I appreciate what you're trying to do, but I'm not interested in starting something new with anyone right now."

Max spit coffee out through his nose. He doubled over, bracing himself on the couch while erupting in laughter. I didn't know if I should have been relieved or insulted.

"What's so funny?" I could feel the heat rising to my cheeks.

"Raven…I'm gay." He was now hunched on the floor holding his side from laughing so hard.

I was mortified. "Oh my god. I'm so sorry. I'm such an idiot." I wrapped my arms around myself and wished I could disappear.

Max plopped down on the couch. "It's okay. I haven't laughed that hard in years. You country girls are so refreshing. Now, you're going to get dressed and accompany me out so you can make it up to me." He had a smug grin on his face.

"Ah, I see what you're doing. Fine. I owe you after that embarrassment. Give me twenty minutes."

He gave me a wink. "Another reason why I like you. A city girl would keep me waiting here for hours."

Exactly twenty-five minutes later, I had showered, changed into a faded pair of jeans, yellow cashmere sweater, and black wedged boots. I threw my dark hair up into a ballerina style bun and applied a light coat of mascara and clear lip gloss.

Max let out a low whistle. "Damn, girl, you clean up nice."

"So what's the plan for today?" Now that I was ready to go, I was actually looking forward to getting out and distracting myself.

"We are going to have a true New York City adventure. First things first, no more cabs. Today you are going to experience the subway."

⁓

We started out with brunch and mimosas at Cafeteria, followed by a walk through Central Park where I fawned over the bronzed Alice in Wonderland statues for a little too long. That was always my favorite book as a child. I used to dream I was Alice and prayed that when I went to sleep, I'd be in Wonderland when I woke up.

We hit the shops on Fifth Avenue—window shopping only as the price tags were way beyond my budget. Then Times Square so he could make fun of all the tourists with their fanny packs and Statue of Liberty tee shirts. Next I coerced him into Dylan's Candy Bar so I could load up on sweets. He laughed and feigned embarrassment as I proceeded to try every gummi candy before purchasing.

The weather was starting to turn with a light rainfall, so we decided it would be the perfect time to check out the Metropolitan Museum of Art. Not only did they have one of the world's largest collections of art, but they also had a bookstore and a restaurant.

"I'm really glad you dragged me out. I'm feeling so much better," I said as we climbed up the main steps.

"There is nothing this city can't cure. Thanks for being my *date* for the day."

I wanted to cringe. "Sorry again about that. I shouldn't have assumed you were into me."

Max chuckled. "It happens. No big deal. I found it hilarious actually and flattering, of course."

I breathed a sigh of relief. The last thing I wanted to do was to offend the only friend I had in New York. "So do you have a boyfriend?"

"I'm seeing someone. He hasn't called in a few days but I'm trying to give myself another twenty four hours before I go into full panic mode."

I shoved him playfully in the arm. "Ah, so it's you that needs the distraction. And here I thought you were trying to help me out," I teased.

He handed money to the ticket salesman for both of us. "Okay maybe I had an ulterior motive. But it's a win-win for both of us."

The museum was enormous. It was like its own city. We spent hours walking from room to room, looking at everything from Picasso paintings to Medieval artifacts, to an actual replica of an Egyptian tomb. It made me long for that summer I spent at Ozi's vineyard in Italy. I wished I could afford to see more of the world.

We parked ourselves on a bench in front of a John Singer Sargent painting—Madame X, it was called. I loved this painting. It was such a mysterious piece, the way the subject is looking away yet her body language faces forward. Like her body was present but her mind was somewhere else. I often felt like that. I wondered what her secrets were. What was she holding back? And that black dress...one of the most gorgeous dresses I'd ever seen and could only dream of wearing.

"So, you want to talk about the phone call you got last night? The one that literally made you run out on a perfectly delicious appletini," Max probed.

I stared at the painting for a minute before answering. I knew that this was going to come up and I couldn't dodge it all day, but I still felt like I was teetering on the edge of crumbling at the mere thought of it. "It was from my ex...he's getting married."

Max puckered his lips into a sad face.

"To my sister." There, I said it out loud.

His shoulders perked up and his face twisted into one of shock and horror. "Ohhh...what the..."

"Yeah, I know, it's fucking weird. That's the kind of shit that happens when you grow up in a small town, I guess."

Max shook his head in disgust. "Girl, that is some sick Freudian bullshit if you ask me. What do your parents think?"

I shrugged and took a sip of the coffee I was still nursing, wincing as it hit my tongue. It was ice cold now. "Nothing really. My sister always got what she wanted. When we were kids, if she liked a doll I got for Christmas better than hers, she would just take it. My parents would never tell her no. I think it was the guilt. She almost died when she was a baby. They coddled her ever since. So when she decided it was my boyfriend she wanted, they didn't object."

Max's eyes were so wide, I thought they might pop out of their sockets. "That's the craziest shit I've ever heard, and I'm from New Jersey. Damn girl, no wonder you left. How long ago did this happen?"

"It's been a year. Now that they are getting married, I'm not going back there ever. That's it. I'm done. It just hurts too much. He was the first boy…the only boy I've ever loved. I didn't just lose him; I lost my family too. I am really alone now." I could feel the tears threatening to well up again. I took another sip of the cold coffee in an attempt to shock my system out of wanting to cry.

Max threw an arm over my shoulder. "I'm sorry, Raven, but you're not alone anymore. I'm glad we met. I'm here for you whenever you need."

"Thank you." I leaned into his shoulder and it felt good. I couldn't remember the last time I had been shown any affection. Even the platonic kind.

"Now, let's go get a drink. My mimosa buzz is wearing off." Max pulled me to my feet and dragged me in the direction of the Met Café.

The place was packed and there was only one space at the bar. As I glanced around the brightly lit café, looking for an empty table, my gaze locked with a familiar face and my stomach did a little somersault. *Ozi.*

Eight

Ozi

"**O**zi, are you listening to me?" Cassius asked. I wasn't. Raven and Max had just walked into the Met Café. *What were the odds?*

I waved toward them. "Yeah—crypto, coding, lots of numbers, all that stuff." I was not a numbers guy.

Cassius snorted. "Sorry that I'm boring you. Who are you waving at?"

"Some of my staff from *Dolce Sale*. I'm inviting them over. Our business is done here, no?"

"Apparently." He stood and stuffed his laptop into a leather bag. "So far, Camille hasn't done anything out of the ordinary. I'll let you know if I find anything else out."

I nodded, keeping my gaze fixated on Raven. "Yeah, yeah. But none of the boring stuff. Just get to the point next time."

Cassius towered over me and scowled. Not only was he large for a man, he was also large for his kind. Cassius was a werewolf, but luckily for me he was a patient one with a long fuse. God knows I've done everything to test him over the years. "Yes, princess, I'll try to make it more palatable for you next time."

"Very funny. Talk soon."

He patted me on the back on his way out, passing Max and Raven on their way over to my table. Cassius paused and turned around to throw me a look. One he's given me before. It meant he took one look at Raven and knew exactly what I was doing. He shook his head as he continued to leave. But not before sending me a quick text.

You cut our meeting short so you could get laid?

I fired back with:

Yes, that's exactly what I did. Now go fuck yourself.

I could just imagine the smirk on his face as he read it. Cassius knew me well and he was one of the few people who could call me out on my shit.

Max bumbled over with a reluctant looking Raven a few steps behind him. "Boss! What are the odds we run into you again? I didn't know you hung out at the Met."

"I have many hidden passions, Max." I winked at Raven. "Nice to see you again. Sorry we didn't have a chance to speak last night at the bar. Thank you again for your excellent service. Please, join me?" The blood raced in my veins. I had to count back from ten in my head to keep my dick from getting hard again. In the bar was one thing, but not in broad daylight.

Raven gripped her coat to her chest like it was a security blanket. "Oh, we don't want to impose."

"Nonsense. My business has finished and there are no other empty tables. Besides, I'd like to buy you both a drink. Get to know each other better. You're all going to be seeing a lot more of me. I have matters that are keeping me in the city much longer than I anticipated." *You are keeping me here. With your hungry green eyes and soft lips.*

Raven inched down into the opposite chair. "You don't live here full-time?"

Max bubbled with excitement. "Mr. Fabiano has a sick house upstate. That's where the real parties are. The other night was nothing compared to those."

I couldn't help but smile. Sometimes I thought everyone else loved my parties more than I did. Especially the staff who worked them. "Please, call me Ozi. And yes, I usually only come into the city once a month. I like the quiet and the space of my estate. The air is cleaner and there are more trees. And yet I'm just a quick helicopter ride away from the city. The best of both worlds you could say."

"Yeah, Mr.—uh, Ozi, has his own helipad. So freaking cool," Max chimed in.

Raven did not look impressed. In fact she wasn't looking at me at all. Instead she was fixated on the menu. Most women wet their panties when they found out how much money I had. This one seemed to be bored by it.

I gently took the menu from her hands. "Do you like champagne?"

She fidgeted with the edge of her yellow cashmere sweater. "We've been drinking mimosas all day, so yes. I love champagne."

"Yes, let's keep it going, girl," Max cooed.

"Excellent," I said. "Let's change it up a little, shall we? I'll order us a round of Bellinis."

Max's phone rang. "Ooh, I have to take this. I'll be right back." He leapt up from the table like it was on fire and stepped out of the café.

Raven nodded and smiled. She looked amazing. "I didn't figure you for a peach Bellini drinker," she teased.

Was that actual sarcasm? Maybe I was wearing her down. I flashed her a grin. "It's all about *la dolce vita*, darling. The sweet life." I signaled to the server, placed the order, and turned my attention back to her. "There are many things that I think will surprise you about me."

Her green eyes sparkled. A hint of intrigue flickered through them. "Everything in moderation right?"

"Depends on what you're indulging in. When it comes to the senses, moderation is overrated. Food, drink, sex...those are pleasures we must enjoy to the fullest." *I wanted to bend her over this table and show her.*

The vein in her neck quivered. "Too much of anything can poison even the sweetest of intentions. There is something to be said for playing it safe. To not lose yourself."

I leaned forward and placed my hand gently over hers. "Sometimes losing yourself is the sweetest part. Until then, you haven't truly lived."

She pulled her hand away. We stared at each other for what seemed like an eternity.

Max hurried back over. "So sorry about that."

"Everything okay?" Raven asked. Her pulse was still unsteady.

"Better than okay. Alfonso finally called. He wants to meet up." Max was glowing with excitement. "But I told him I have plans with my country girl."

Raven playfully smacked him in the arm. "Are you nuts? You've been talking about him all day. You have to call him back. I can get home by myself."

"Are you sure? You're still not familiar with the city," Max said.

I jumped in. "Max, you should go. Don't you worry about Raven. I'll look after her." *I certainly wanted to do more than just look.*

Raven fidgeted with her sleeve again. "Yes, I'm sure. Now get out of here before Alfonso makes other plans."

Max jumped up and kissed her on the cheek. "I'll text you later." He reached for his wallet and I shooed his hand away. "Thanks, boss. Make sure this one gets home eventually." He winked.

She rolled her eyes at him but giggled as he ambled off.

"Well, Raven. It's just you and me now. What do you say we indulge in one of those senses?" I let my glass linger against my lips, pushing out the tip of my tongue to meet the peach infused champagne.

Her breath quickened. "I—um..." She looked like she was going to bolt for the nearest exit.

I chuckled. "Relax, darling. I'm talking about food. You will join me for dinner, yes? My treat."

Raven let out a deep breath of relief. "I'm not sure if that's a good idea. I mean… I work for you. What will people think?"

Watching her squirm was more entertaining than I thought it would be. "And yet we've just had drinks together. I'm not asking for your hand in marriage, just dinner between friends. Besides, it's a big city, Raven. The odds of anyone from *Dolce Sale* seeing us is very slim. I personally don't care if they do, but if that is a concern of yours, I understand. So…will you join me?"

Raven

I wasn't sure if it was the champagne buzz or the high from seeing priceless works of art. Or maybe it was his full lips and perfectly smooth skin, or the way he smelled—like the night. Maybe it was all of it, but I was entranced. I should have left. I should have done a lot of things differently that day. But I stayed.

"I'm not dressed for dinner." I looked down at my jeans and thought as cute as they were, they weren't exactly five star attire.

Ozi was not phased. "It's settled then. I'll swing you by your place. You can change while I call ahead and let them know we're coming."

"Okay. But I want to make myself clear. This isn't a date." I was actually excited. I didn't want him to think it was a date but I was looking forward to getting dressed up and going out.

Alex and I only went out on special occasions like my birthday or our anniversary. At least in the beginning. Three years into our relationship, we stopped going out altogether. He'd said it was because being at home was cozier, but it was more about him being able to watch sports on TV while I waited on him hand and foot. I loved cooking but every once in a while, it would be nice to have food cooked for me. Besides, he was such a picky eater, it was always just pasta or hamburgers. My palate always craved more.

Ozi paid the bill at the Met café and offered me his hand. "This will be the best non-date you've ever had."

When we pulled up in front of my apartment, I didn't invite him in and he didn't insist. As I turned the key to my place, my insecurities set in. What in the hell was I doing? He was my boss and one of the richest men in New York City. Why out of all people did he want to have dinner with me? Was he bored?

I loved that Piper had an old school answering machine. The light was blinking and it reminded me of one of those outdated movies when the girl comes home to check if anyone actually likes her enough to call and leave a message.

I pushed the blinking button and Piper's bubbly voice came pouring out.

'Hi, Raven. I hope you're settling in! So sorry to abandon you on your first week in the city but my boss has me working overtime and it looks like I'm not going to make it home for a bit longer. My house is your house. Help yourself to whatever and I hope to see you soon. Can't wait to hear all about your adventures! Ciao for now.'

Anything I wanted? I wasn't the most fashion savvy and Maplewood wasn't exactly the epicenter of haute couture. Against my better judgement, I found myself in Piper's closet. If I was going to go out to dinner with one of the most eligible bachelors in the free world, I at least needed to look the part.

Looking in the mirror, I barely recognized myself. I decided on a black lace dress that stopped just below my knees and hugged every curve. The sleeves were three-quarter and the neckline plunged just low enough to show a peek of cleavage without revealing too much. I had no idea what I was doing and for the first time, I didn't care. I was going to try to live that city life. I didn't move here to play it safe.

By the way Ozi staggered back against the town car, I could tell I had made the right choice. His lips curled into a smirk as he opened the door for me.

"You look…amazing. Are you sure this isn't a date?"

"It's not." The way he looked at me was unnerving. It wasn't just the dress. It was as if he could see through me and into the deepest parts of me.

"Whatever you want to call it is fine with me, Raven, but I can't promise you that you won't be able to keep your hands off me by the end of the night."

I swallowed hard and he winked.

"I'll try to contain myself."

And then he laughed, followed by the most sincere and warmest smile I'd ever seen from any other human being.

Maybe I was better at this than I thought.

Nine

Raven

I SHOULDN'T BE HERE. I SHOULDN'T BE THIS CLOSE TO HIM. The way he looked at me…like I was on the menu. His fingers stroked the rim of his whiskey glass and I imagined what that would feel like on my skin. How his fingers would feel between my legs and in my mouth. His gaze burned into mine, imploring, seeking, hungry. He wanted me. Why? What was so special about me? I didn't care. I wanted him too. I shouldn't. He was my boss and so out of my league. For fuck's sake, his suit cost more than my rent. Why did I agree to this?

"Tell me what you're thinking. I can see your thoughts are heavy." Ozi dipped his finger into his glass and brought it to his lips, using just the tip of his tongue to lick it clean.

My belly tingled under the heat of his stare. "I was just wondering what I'm doing here…with you. You could have dinner with anyone you want. Why me?"

"You are correct. I can choose anyone I want, so I choose you." It was getting harder to look him in the eye when all I could do was stare at his fingers tracing the rim of the glass. I wanted to see him lick them again. My god, what was wrong with me? This wasn't like me. Sweat dripped down my thighs as the heat in my body turned up several notches.

"Yes, but why me?"

Every glance I took from him made me feel like I was on fire.

He leaned back in his chair. The vein in his neck twitched. "Why not you, Raven?"

"Um, I don't understand the question." He was teasing me and all I could think about was climbing over this table to straddle him.

"I just thought we should get to know each other better. First the winery, now *Dolce Sale*, you seem to keep finding your way to me… I mean my company, of course." He winked and took a slow seductive sip of his drink.

I shrugged. "Coincidence."

"Fate."

Oh, he was good.

I shifted in my chair, feeling more vulnerable than ever. "I don't believe in fate."

Ozi laughed softly. "Things exist with or without belief. It doesn't make them any less true," he drawled. "Tell me, Raven, what brings you to New York City? You are a long way from home, no?"

This was exactly the conversation I did not want to have. The reason I needed to keep my distance from him. It was an innocent question, but he would not be satisfied with my answer. Ozi was a man who was used to getting what he wanted and he was going to push until he did. "When I was in Italy, interning at your winery, I discovered my passion for food. For cooking. I decided then I wanted to become a chef."

Ozi leaned forward and I caught a whiff of his cologne—a mixture of tobacco and sandalwood. A tingly sensation rippled through me. *Damn pheromones.*

"You could not become a chef in Maplewood?"

I almost choked on my wine. "Have you ever been to Maplewood?" I asked. "Maybe if I wanted to flip burgers all day or master the grilled cheese sandwich. So yeah, no. I want to be a real chef in a five-star restaurant. And someday have my own restaurant…like you."

He watched me so closely, like he was analyzing my every movement. "So you left all your family and friends behind to become a chef? I admire that. I'll tell Enzo to give you a couple shifts in the kitchen."

The music changed to a deeper, more tribal beat. I felt my heart race against it. "Look, no disrespect, but I don't want any special favors. I need to do this on my own."

Ozi's eyes lit up with amusement. "You work for me, Raven. I can put you in any position I want."

I held my breath as his words conjured up an image of him bending me over the back of this chair. "Um…"

"I'm speaking about the restaurant, of course. Unless you had something else in mind." He leaned forward and placed his hand over mine. The heat from his skin sent shivers up my back. My god, what was happening to me?

I snatched my hand away. "Let's keep this professional."

He laughed. "I'm only joking. I would never cross the line. I like to help all my employees achieve their dreams in my restaurant. Max started out as a food runner, now he's one of the top bartenders in New York City. If you would like to try out the kitchen, the opportunity is there for you."

"I'd appreciate that. Thank you," I stammered.

"Excellent." He raised his glass. "Here's to you pursuing your dreams, and me possibly getting a new chef." He winked and clanked my glass.

"Cheers."

"*Saluti.*"

I couldn't help but notice the whispers and stares from the tables around us. Ozi was practically famous in this city and they were probably wondering what he was doing here with someone so small time like me. The staff, on the other hand, fawned all over us. They brought us course after course of raw oysters, seared foie gras on crusted bread, steaming bowls of lobster bisque, caprese salads with pastel colored heirloom tomatoes and fresh burrata. The main course was just as decadent. We had filet mignon in a blackberry wine reduction. Though the portions were small, the food was so rich and luxurious, I thought my belly would burst.

The white-gloved server placed an extravagant plate of dessert bites in between us—macarons, petit fours, truffles, and profiteroles. "Oh, wow. I can't possibly—"

"You must. Juliet's pastries are world famous. I've been trying to poach their pastry chef for years." He bit into a dark chocolate truffle and golden caramel oozed out and onto his lips. He closed his eyes as he licked at it, chewing slow to savor every bite.

"If I put anything else in my mouth, you're going to have to carry me out of here," I teased.

"That can be arranged. Close your eyes." His voice was low and breathy.

I hesitated, looking around to see who was watching us now. "I…I really shouldn't."

"Trust me, Raven. You won't regret it." He smiled, dangling the chocolate near my lips.

I shuddered. Every inch of my skin was tingling, the hairs on my arms raised. He gazed into my eyes as if he could see deep into my soul. "Trust has to be earned," I murmured.

He inched closer—the half-bitten truffle so close, I could smell the sweet buttery caramel. "This is how it begins."

My breath caught in my throat. I wanted to taste it more than anything. The music pulsed around us, a melody of haunting violins and crashing cymbals. My heart fluttered as I gave in and closed my eyes.

"Open your mouth, Raven." His voice was sensual and seductive.

I did as he said and parted my lips. The sweet gooey caramel slid across my tongue and as he nudged the truffle into my mouth, the tip of his finger grazed my lip. It sent a tingling sensation all the way down to the wet spot between my thighs.

I wanted more—more dark chocolate, more luscious caramel. More of his sticky sweet touch. I felt like I was losing my mind. When I opened my eyes, reality set back in. The whispers intensified and one table even snickered as they watched us. Yet Ozi only fixated on me. But no matter what the onlookers assumed, there was no way I was going to sleep with him tonight.

Ozi

I would break her down and make her surrender. Make her beg for it.

The way she licked her lips…it took everything I had not to throw her over this table and fuck her till she could barely stand. If I had any wonder about her wanting me too, well, I didn't have to wonder anymore. She was timid and it was clear that she had never known true pleasure before. Love, perhaps, but not true pleasures of the flesh.

Fuck those who gawked at us. Let them whisper. They were just jealous. Most humans were. I had her right where I wanted her—literally eating out of the palm of my hand. I didn't give a shit about the rules or Enzo or even that she worked for me. I was a predator. Once I got a whiff of her scent, I couldn't stop hunting her even if I wanted to.

After paying the check, I stood and rushed to help her with her coat. Monster or not, I was still a gentleman. "Let's swing by my place before I take you home. I have a limited reserve Bordeaux I want you to taste."

Raven leaned back on her high heels and arched an eyebrow at me. "I don't think that's a good idea. Maybe another time."

My heart raced. "So there *will* be a next time?" *I'll take that as a win.* "Come on, darling. Let's get you home." I didn't expect it would be that easy to get her into my bed, but it was worth a try. I had a feeling she wouldn't be so quick to crack. That excited me all the more.

We pulled up in front of her place and she lingered in my car. "Thank you for a really nice night. The food was amazing and the company was…surprising."

"How so?" I was curious to understand how her mind ticked.

She blushed and reached for the door handle. "You were more of a gentleman than I thought you'd be."

I laughed. "Just say the word and I can change that. In all seriousness, Raven, this was a true pleasure. And I meant what I said, I will help you any way I can in your dreams to become a chef."

She looked back and her eyelids fluttered. I couldn't move. She had me frozen in place under her stare. Without warning, she slid closer to me across the leather seats. The carnal hunger clawed at me and I willed myself to not devour her. With her fragile fingers, she traced my lips. I let out a soft quiver and tried with all my power to restrain myself.

"What are you doing?" I whispered.

She looked up at me with her big green eyes and shook her head. "I don't know. But I've been wanting to do that all night."

I clasped her hands in mine and drew them down into my lap. "What do you want right now?"

She licked her lips as she eyed me. "I…I had too much to drink. I'm sorry. I should go." But she didn't budge.

I leaned forward. Her hands were still inside mine and our lips were just inches apart. Her pulse raced. "Tell me to stop and I will," I whispered.

She didn't make a sound as she closed her eyes. The roundness of her lips puckered toward me and I had to push down the guttural growl that threatened to escape. I was going to claim her. She whimpered at the tickle of my breath on her neck as I inhaled her scent, letting my lips hover over her ear. "*Tell me to stop*," I pleaded.

Without warning, she pressed her lips to mine. She was warm

and sweet and I lost it. I pushed my tongue insider her mouth and she moaned. I had never seen a woman react like that from just a kiss.

But it ended as quickly as it had started. She squeezed my shoulders and nudged me back, gasping for air.

My dick was harder than a rock and all I could think about was draining her dry. But somehow she managed to reign me in. She held me in place with just her gaze.

"I'm—I'm sorry. I can't do this." Without another word or glance she leapt out of my car and bolted up the stairs to her apartment.

I sank back into the leather seats, shuddering. *What the fuck just happened?* I cupped my swollen dick in my hands and willed my heartbeat to slow down. In over a hundred years, I had never met any woman who could have her way with me like that.

Ten

Raven

I SLID DOWN THE TERRA COTTA TILED SHOWER WALL AND LET the cold water rain over me. The tears gushed down my cheeks like a dam breaking. What in the hell had come over me back there? I let him kiss me. *I kissed him*. What was wrong with me? Just because Alex was getting married didn't mean I had to go make out with the first man who showed me affection. That's not who I was. But…Ozi. He did something to me. Stirred something inside of me that I thought was dead.

I was mortified. I drank too much and made a pass at my boss. How was I ever going to face him again? To make matters worse, I kissed him and then ran like a confused teenager. He must think I'm such a mess. I wrapped myself up in my robe and made a cup of tea. Just as the bag was almost finished steeping, the light blinked on my phone.

It was a text from an unknown number:

> *We need to talk, darling.*

Shit. He didn't waste any time. He probably wanted to take back his offer about helping me and fire me altogether. I can't believe how unprofessional I acted. Sure he flirted with me first, but I took the bait and literally ran away with it.

I thought for a second and then texted back:

> *Of course. Again, I'm sorry for my unprofessional behavior tonight.*

A couple minutes went by. Without thinking, I took a gulp of my steaming hot tea and burned my tongue. *Dammit.* I was not myself. My phone light flashed.

> *I'm at your door.*

Oh dear god. *This can't be happening.* He must really want to get this over with. How could I blame him? There wasn't any time to change. I tucked the strap of my robe in tight and tip-toed to the door.

"Open the door, Raven," Ozi called out.

My heart was practically in my throat, beating so fast I could barely breathe.

I opened the door. "Have you been outside this whole time?" I asked.

He pushed past me and invited himself in. "We circled around the block a few times…I couldn't go home without speaking to you again."

I hugged my arms to my chest. The dampness from my hair was starting to chill the back of my neck. "Look, about the kiss…I don't know what came over me. I don't want to lead you on or—"

"Stop, Raven. Just stop. You know exactly what came over you. We both do." He crossed the room and backed me up against the kitchen wall. "The question I have is, why did you run away?"

I gazed up at his dark brown eyes. A part of me wanted to surrender and another part of me wanted to hide. "Because it was a mistake. I can't go there with you. You're my boss and I'm not…I'm not looking to get involved with anyone right now. I just can't."

Ozi inched closer to me, our noses almost touching. "You're already involved with me. Whether you like it or not, you made that decision back in my car. There's no going back from that now." He gently squeezed the tie of my robe, using it to tug me forward till my hips were nestled against his. Shivers raced down my thighs. He whispered in my ear, "Maybe not tonight, or tomorrow, but we will finish this. *I will have you.*"

I wanted him to take me right there. To hoist me onto his hips and take me hard against this wall. I whimpered at the thought of it.

His lips curled into a half-smirk, half-snarl, and for a split second I could have sworn his eyes glowed in the dim light of my apartment. He sniffed my hair, shuddering as he inhaled my scent. "You intoxicate me. Your absence *starves* me. When I'm near you, I ache to taste you." His soft lips tickled my earlobe. I couldn't move. I didn't want to. He had me pinned. "And I always get what I want, Raven. *Always.*" There was something predatory about him in that moment. A wild streak in his eyes that was almost inhuman.

"You—you should go." If he stayed any longer, I was going to give in and let him do what he wanted with me. And when things didn't work out, as they normally don't, I'd have to look for a new job and possibly even a new city to live in. A man like Ozi didn't seem like the type that was easy to get over. My wounds were still so fresh they didn't even have scars yet. Fucking Ozi would be like pouring salt on them.

Ozi chuckled. "I know that's not what you want but I'll obey. But don't fool yourself, *darling*...one of these nights soon, you will be begging for me to fuck you sideways."

A whimper escaped my throat as he released me. I pulled my robe closer to my chest, relieved but also wishing he hadn't let go.

He waltzed to the door, pausing at it without looking back. "I *will* break you."

"You can't break what's already broken," I murmured back.

The door shut with a thud behind him and I collapsed onto the hardwood floor like a rag doll. My whole body trembled. Everything about him was dark and dangerous, but all I could think about was how much I wanted more of him.

Ozi

My head was spinning. I needed blood and a cold shower. I had half my collar unbuttoned when I sensed her presence before I even turned the key to my penthouse. Every hair on the back of my neck stood straight up.

Camille draped herself across my couch. "You've been a bad boy, Ozi. Fraternizing with humans again."

This bitch had a lot of nerve. "How did you get in here?"

"I'm a vampire, remember? Your security measures are pathetic." She lifted a bottle of my finest scotch to her lips and took a long pull.

"What do you want, Camille? I'm not in the mood for your games." I was half-tempted to toss her off the terrace.

She scooted down and spread her legs apart, nestling the bottle between them. "You used to love to play with me, my love. Seeing you with that fragile girl tonight…well, it made me jealous."

"So you're spying on me now? I swear if you go anywhere near her, I'll—"

"Relax, lover. I'm not that vindictive. Or am I?" She let out a sadistic laugh.

I grabbed her by the arms and lifted her up, pushing her back into the wall. "Don't you forget who you're dealing with. I'm not the one to fuck with, Camille. Tell me what you're really here for and then get the fuck out." Her skin was starting to redden under my fingers. Yet it would take a lot more than that if I wanted to hurt her. Immortal creatures weren't easily wounded. At least not physically that is. Emotionally…that was a different thing altogether. And she was clearly still wounded over what happened between us centuries ago.

She didn't flinch and her icy blue eyes hardened with that steel piercing gaze she was so good at throwing my way. "Take your hands off me, Ozi, or the next thing you touch will be pieces of your new girl-friend's body."

I growled and could feel the tips of my fangs protruding out. I still needed to feed and now I was overwhelmed by this insatiable need to protect Raven at all costs. I released Camille from my hands and reached for the bottle of scotch, downing the rest of it before coming up for air.

"She means nothing to me. Just a girl I want to fuck next. So save the dramatics and tell me what you want. I'm tired and hungry and about two strides away from snapping your neck."

Camille strutted to the door, picking up her fur coat and purse from the couch as she did. "I just came as a courtesy. To let you know I've purchased a restaurant of my own. I'll be staying in New York in-definitely. Hope that's not going to be a problem?"

Fuck. "Stay as long as you like, Camille. Just keep out of my way and my life. Whether you forgive me for the past or not, we both know I have paid enough for what I did. Open ten restaurants for all I care."

She batted her eyelashes at me like an innocent little girl, but I knew better. She was far from innocent and she always had an ulterior motive. Her stiletto heels clicked, echoing across my marble floors as she walked toward the door. "Bye for now, Ozi. Oh and you might want to get a better security system. I'm sure I'm not the only other vampire who you've crossed in your infinite days. *Ciao.*"

Her perfume lingered in the air—Chanel No. 5. Some things never changed. She always did have good taste. Expensive taste. I charged toward the kitchen and scrambled open the safe—one of many safes I owned all over the city. I couldn't get the blood bag opened fast enough. I had gone too long tonight. The chilled blood was refreshing, despite the fact that it tasted nothing like it did when it was fresh from the vein.

I slumped into a chair on the patio and gazed out at the city while I drained three more blood bags. Camille was nothing like she was when we first met. That was my fault probably. But she never loved me. Not before the change and not after. Otherwise she wouldn't have rejected me when she learned what I was. I don't think anyone can really love that much anyway. So I couldn't blame her. I was asking her to love a monster and when she refused, I turned her into one. There were times she was scarier than me. And that was saying a lot. But Raven didn't belong mixed up in all this. She was a sweet girl from a small town with big dreams.

Enzo was right, I needed to stay away from her. But after that kiss…I didn't see how that was going to be possible.

Eleven

Raven

THE COOKS IN THE KITCHEN OF *DOLCE SALE* STARED AT ME LIKE
I had two heads. Watching Enzo explain to them that I would be
training as a cook was comical. I understood enough Italian to
know that they were not happy about *country girl* invading their space.
Head chef, Arturo, glared at me like I had just stolen his knives.

"Enzo, are you sure this is okay? I don't want to upset anyone." I
already felt like an outsider enough.

"*Si, si.* They hate change but they'll get used to it. I have no doubt
you will win them over just as you have done with Ozi." Enzo handed
me a white chef coat and left me standing alone with four angry
Italians. If one of them broke the bechamel sauce it would be my fault.

Arturo pointed at the prep station and grumbled something I
could barely understand. Something that sounded like *mirepoix*. I had
read enough to know that was a mixture of diced carrots, onions, and

celery. I tied my hair back, took a deep breath, and started chopping. Within minutes, he stomped over and yanked the knife out of my hand. "*Basta*. Stop," he yelled. "No, watch. Like this." The way he moved the knife in and out, slicing and dicing, like a dance, it was amazing he didn't sever a finger. I followed his lead and after a few more tries and more yelling, I got the hang of it. I wasn't as fast as him, but at least I was starting to get the technique down. And the red in his cheeks began to dissipate. I thought he was going to burst a vein in his neck at one point. If he threw me out of the kitchen, my career as a chef would be over before it even began.

The tension between me and the cooks was starting to subside as we fell into a rhythm. I stayed out of their way and did what I was told. I'd always been a fast learner and I was good at being quiet. When I was a kid, I'd go days without speaking sometimes, just wrapped up in my books. Alex was the one who had drawn me out of my shell. Ironic that he was the reason I retreated back into it.

I worked in the kitchen for the next three nights. On night four, Chef Arturo felt confident enough to let me move off of prep and onto the sauce station. I still had to serve in the dining room the other two nights of the week but being in the kitchen made it worth it. I could literally see my dreams materializing. Visions of running my own kitchen filled my head. But I had a long way to go. I never went to culinary school so it would take me a lot longer to get my skills up to par with the chefs in this industry.

Tonight we were hustling. It was Friday and we were slammed. But the promise that I could have the weekend off kept me going. Working in the kitchen came with a nice raise that made up for the loss of tips on the floor. I'd been working my ass off and was looking for a little self-care wine weekend alone. Although, I did promise Max I'd have brunch with him on Sunday.

The rowdy kitchen fell to a hush. I looked up to see Ozi staring back at me. Arturo ran over to him and shook his hand. They conversed back and forth in Italian, so fast I could only pick up every other word. They liked and respected each other. That was evident from the wide grins on their faces and their relaxed body language. Arturo kept his hand on Ozi's shoulder while he talked. Then he ushered him over to a large pot and shoveled a heaping spoon of Bolognese sauce into his mouth. Ozi's eyes lit up as he swallowed.

"*Ti piace?*" Arturo asked. "Do you like?"

Ozi patted him on the back. "*Si*, Arturo. *Molto bene.* Delicious as always."

"*Grazie.* Thank you." Arturo beamed with pride like a child who had just received a gold star.

Ozi towered over me but I didn't dare look up again. I continued to stir the bechamel I was working on for the truffle mac and cheese.

"*Ciao*, Raven. They treating you good back here?" His voice was silky and laced with desire. Images of his breath on my neck, his lips against mine, flashed through my mind, making me light headed.

I glanced over at Arturo who was watching us intently. "Great actually." Arturo let out a sigh of relief and went back to plating. "I'm learning so much."

Ozi smiled wide and dipped his finger in the sauce. He sucked it off slow. He closed his eyes as he savored it. "Wow, Raven. This...this tastes *perfecto.*"

Despite the nerves fluttering in my chest, I was pleased that he liked my sauce. Ozi was a perfectionist. That's why his restaurants were award winning. "Thank you," I murmured.

Enzo rushed in. "The vans are loaded and ready to go for tomorrow, *signore*. I'll ride with the staff as usual."

Ozi nodded and gave me a wink. "See you tomorrow night, Raven."

Wait. What? He dashed out before I could respond. I arched an eyebrow at Enzo. "What did he mean by that?"

"Ozi's party is tomorrow night. At his country estate. Didn't you get the email I sent you?"

Email? Now we were being formal? I don't even remember giving him my email address. The world I came from did not prepare me for this one. "Um…" I bit my lip.

Enzo burst out laughing. "I'm only kidding, Raven. There was no email. When you work for Ozi, you have to be prepared to change shifts at a moment's notice. We will be catering a party at his house tomorrow night. It's a bit of a drive so we always spend the night. The van will pick you up at eleven am sharp." He helped himself to a spoonful of sauce. "Mmm, delicious."

The rest of the night was a blur. After breaking down my station, I clocked out and hailed a cab. I still didn't feel comfortable taking the subway at night by myself. Ugh. This was the last thing I wanted to happen. Not only was I not getting the weekend off like I'd planned, but I was going to have to spend the night at Ozi's house. I called Max on my way home.

"We're still doing brunch on Sunday, right?" Max spurted out before even saying hello.

"Well, I guess that depends on when we get back. Have you ever been to Ozi's other house before? Where are we going to sleep?"

"We usually have a slumber party in Ozi's room. We feed him grapes and take turns massaging each other." Max snorted, but it took me a few minutes to realize he was joking.

"Very funny. Seriously though, what kind of party is this?" Before I kissed Ozi, I never would have questioned it. Now I was as nervous as I was on my first day.

"Just more of the same. Don't worry, girl. It will be fun. He has a guest house that we all crash in and we usually get the leftover caviar and champagne. We have our own party after the suits go to sleep." The excitement in his voice was palpable.

"Okay…I guess I don't have a choice. I'll see ya tomorrow."

Max made an exaggerated kissy noise into the phone that made me lurch back. "Sorry, I've been drinking. All right, girl, sweet dreams. And we *are* still doing brunch on Sunday. It's my favorite meal of the day. Byeee." He hung up laughing.

The cab driver cleared his throat. "Pardon me, Miss, but I couldn't help but overhear you. A word of advice. If you are working one of Ozi's parties…keep your head down and be discreet. Some of the most high profile people in the city will be there doing things that they aren't going to want anyone else to know about."

I swallowed hard. I nodded and looked out the window, avoiding the driver's inquisitive eyes on me in the mirror. *What in the hell have I gotten myself into?*

◦◦◦

The answering machine was blinking like a beacon in the dark. I locked the door behind me, kicked off my shoes and went straight for the wine cabinet. After pouring a large glass of Bordeaux and slicing up a few of the artisan cheeses that were in the fridge, I leaned up against the wall and hit the message button. I still couldn't believe that Piper had an actual answering machine. And I was from Maplewood, the smallest town on the planet. Even we had moved on from those.

"*You have two messages,*" the automated voice stated.

"*Piper, it's Harley. I have that info you asked for. You're probably half way to someplace crazy like the Bermuda triangle by now, so I'll try you on your burner. If you're checking remotely, delete this message.*"

So that was weird. Piper has a burner phone? And who the heck is Harley?

Next message.

"*Hey, Raven! I hope you are settling in and you have everything you need. Sorry again about running off on you but I'm swamped with work. Give me a call when you get a chance. I left a different number in the junk drawer. Talk to ya soon!*"

That must be the burner phone number. Maybe I've watched too many spy movies, but I thought only secret agents and criminals needed one of those. I was seriously starting to question my life choices as I guzzled my wine like it was water. Even though Piper was from

Maplewood, I really knew nothing about her. Now she was getting cryptic messages and asking me to call her on a burner phone? Then there was the fact that I worked for one of the most powerful men in New York City who threw spur of the moment parties and expected his staff to be at his beck and call. For fuck's sake, even the cab driver knew who he was.

I poured another glass of wine and rifled through the kitchen drawers, looking for the one that Piper considered *junk*. It wasn't hard to find. All the other drawers were empty except the one with the plastic ware. For as much money as she'd put into this place, I was getting the impression that she didn't spend much time here. The number was on a yellow sticky note that I had to peel off a buy one get one free pizza coupon.

I dialed the number hesitantly and Piper picked up on the third ring. "Hi, Raven! Thanks for calling me back. How's everything going?"

"Uh, how did you know it was me?" I chuckled.

"Oh, you're the only one who has this number. Everything okay?" She sounded concerned.

"Yeah everything is fine. You had a message from someone named Harley. She said something about calling you on a burner? Are *you* okay?"

Piper let out a nervous laugh. "Don't worry about me, Raven. I have multiple phones for work. Harley just likes to be dramatic. So tell me everything! Did you find a job? Are you settling into the apartment all right?"

Where do I even begin? I didn't know Piper well enough to open up, but I *was* staying at her place. "I'm working at *Dolce Sale*. It's been good. The owner is a bit unusual. He's got us working some party at his upstate house tomorrow night. But he's giving me an opportunity to train as a cook in the kitchen so I can't complain. And I love your apartment, Piper. I feel really comfortable here."

There was a moment of silence and I thought the call had dropped. "Piper?"

"Uh, yeah, I'm still here… So you're working for Ozi?"

My stomach dropped. There was an uncertainty in her voice that wasn't there before. "Do you know him?" I asked.

"Not personally, but I know what he does. Raven…just be careful around him. He's a powerful man who's used to getting what he wants. Don't let him take advantage of you."

Did he have a reputation for sleeping with his staff? Why would she warn me about him? "What do you know about him, Piper?"

Another long pause. "I gotta go, Raven. Just please keep your guard up around him. That's all I can say for now."

She hung up before I could respond. I almost got the impression that someone was next to her. Someone she didn't want listening to our conversation. Between the burner phones, the fancy apartment, and now the warning about Ozi, I was beginning to wonder just what kind of world Piper lived in.

As I tucked myself into bed, I replayed our conversation over again in my head. There *was* something dangerous about Ozi, but that could just be the billionaire vibe he gave off. Either way, I couldn't stop thinking about him and our kiss. But the way he showed up at my apartment without asking, the way he pinned me against the wall with that feral look in his eyes, it made me shiver with both fear and excitement. No man had ever pushed my buttons like that before. As I drifted off to sleep, his parting words echoed through the stillness of the room…

I will break you.

Twelve

Ozi

WE BROUGHT OUT THE GOOD LINENS, THE EXPENSIVE CHINA, and the real crystal. The back yard was tented and lined with paper lanterns and white twinkle lights. This party had to be spectacular. All of my associates would be attending as well as potential investors.

Raven would be here too… I felt this need to impress her. To show her what my money could provide. Though, I had never met a woman less impressed by wealth than her. It was refreshing, but that still didn't stop me from wanting to try. However, I made myself scarce when Enzo showed up with the vans. Something about the thought of her was dangerous. Camille was back in town, lurking, and Raven was an innocent woman with no idea what kind of monster I really was.

"Mr. Ozi, Mr. Cassius is waiting for you in the study," my doorman stated.

Ah Cassius. Nothing like an introverted werewolf to dampen my mood with talk of numbers and eternal doom.

I snatched a bottle of whiskey from the cellar first and then made my way to the study. "Please tell me you've fixed our little hacker problem," I said as I entered.

Cassius sat on the edge of my desk, drink already in hand. "I've never seen anything like it. I have my best people working on it and we cannot circumvent this guy." His long sandy blond hair was tied up into a top knot on his head.

I loosened my tie and sank into one of the leather chairs. "For fuck's sake, Cassius, we need to figure this out, or close that account."

"We can't close it. There are too many moving parts. Too many threads. For now, all I can do is counter block and redirect."

"I have no idea what you're talking about but that sounds like it will have to do for now." I hated talking about these things. Cassius was the brains behind our operation, Lux was the muscle, and I was the pretty face with the charming accent that our investors loved to party with. We balanced each other well. There was one other member once. But we don't talk about him anymore. He couldn't handle the life and went rogue. That was a long time ago.

"So is that pretty girl from the Met going to be here tonight?" Cassius smirked.

"You mean my employee? Yes, she's working the party tonight." I did my best to downplay it.

"I know you too well, brother. She means more to you than that. I think it's about time that a woman got under your skin for more than five minutes."

Oh I definitely want her under me. "Don't get your dick hard, Cassius. Maybe if you actually used it for fucking once in a while, you wouldn't be so obsessed with my sex life."

He pinched his brows together into a scowl. "Fuck you. You know I can't."

"You can't, or you won't? It's been five years since she... Look, all

I'm saying is that you should consider finding a new mate. It's in your nature. If you wait too long, you are going to hurt someone or yourself." Werewolves who were mated were less feral and more controlled. Cassius had been single for a long time and as collected as he seemed, he was a wild animal simmering, just waiting to lose his shit.

Cassius snickered. "Aw, Ozi, you worried about me?"

"Every fucking full moon I worry about you."

The corner of his lips turned down. "I'm fine, Ozi. What you should worry about is Camille and keeping her away from Raven. If she detects even the slightest interest on your part, she'll use her to torture you."

The twinge in my gut told me he was right but compartmentalizing the two was no easy task. I wanted Raven in my bed. I also wanted her to remain unharmed. How was I supposed to reconcile both?

"Enough talk. I don't need to be in a foul mood at my own party. Just forget about all that for tonight. Have a few drinks, mingle, and try to enjoy yourself for once. All work and no play makes for a very dull wolf." I slipped out the door before he had a chance to continue wallowing.

The *Dolce Sale* staff was bustling about but I had yet to lay eyes on Raven. I scanned the rooms as I made my way through the house. I figured she'd be in the kitchen but when I approached the door, I knew she clearly was not. Judging by the conversation two of the girls were having about Raven, she was nowhere near the kitchen. I lingered in the doorway to eavesdrop.

"What's up with country girl? She's so weird," one of the girls said.

"Right? She obviously knows food and wine but she's so socially awkward. Have you seen her at a table? She looks like a robot who can't process human emotion." The other girl giggled.

"Yeah until she waited on Ozi. Did you see how flustered she got? I thought the poor girl was going to drop the wine in his lap."

"Poor country girl."

They both laughed.

81

These fucking idiots. I charged in. "Am I paying you two to gossip?"

They stared at me dumbfounded, their cheeks reddening.

"Well? Do you think you're better than her? Do you think your clothes and your connections make you better than her? Please enlighten me." I was fuming.

The taller blond girl, Tori, stammered first, "Um, we're sorry Mr. Fabiano. We didn't mean to—"

"Let me make myself clear. If I catch you two talking shit about Raven again, I will fire both of you and make sure neither of you work in any decent restaurant ever again. And stop calling her country girl. It's condescending and frankly shows your ignorance. And ladies, ignorance is not attractive." I wanted to slice open their necks and drain them dry. I wanted to see them whimper and plead for their lives while their blood pooled onto my Italian tiled floor.

Tori looked down as she shoved her hands into her apron pockets. "Of course. I am so sorry. It will never happen again."

I didn't even realize I was clenching my fists until the other girl's gaze landed on them. "Good. Now get back to work."

I stormed out, leaving the two girls standing in my kitchen in a state of shock. I was furious. The thought of anyone harming Raven made me want to break a window. Unfortunately, I may have just made things worse for her.

Raven

This house was like a maze. Why did one man need so many rooms? Enzo tasked me with fetching more wine from the cellar but his directions were less than helpful. *Go down the stairs* he'd said. Only problem was there were three different staircases. I assumed they all led to the same place but who knew how many rooms would be down there. If it were anything like the main level, it would be another sprawl of endless doors and corridors.

The stairs were steep and the lighting was muted. Great. I wouldn't put it past me to trip and fall. I ran my hand along the brick wall as I winded down. The bricks were cool and musty under my sweaty palms.

At the ground level, as I suspected, a long corridor full of multiple door options presented itself to me. I tried the first two but they were locked. *Shit.* They were going to send a search party after me if I didn't bring this wine back soon. I turned another doorknob and it opened. I peered in and spotted some oak barrels. This must've been it. I stepped in hesitantly, unsure. The temperature dropped about twenty degrees.

It was a spacious room but if there was wine in here, it must have been hidden because I couldn't see a bottle in sight. I circled around, confused. *What was the purpose of this room?* Against the wall there was one of those coolers that looked like you would store ice cream in. I went over and flinched as I looked down into it. It was filled with IV bags…bags filled with blood. A chill raced up my spine and the hairs prickled on the back of my neck.

"What are you doing in here?"

I spun around and came face to face with Ozi. I froze.

"Raven, I asked you a question. Answer me." His voice was gruff and his eyes wild.

"I—um…I was looking for the wine cellar. I got lost." I didn't dare ask him what he was doing with all that blood.

His eyes hardened. "You're not supposed to be down here. No one is. This room is off limits."

"I didn't know. I'm sorry. I'll go." I stepped around him and proceeded to the door when he caught my wrist.

"You can't tell anyone about what you saw down here." His grip tightened when I didn't immediately respond.

I hated secrets. I stepped toward him with a fury. "I was sent to get wine. It's not my fault Enzo gave me bad directions. If you don't want anyone seeing you have a blood fetish, then you should keep this door locked."

He grabbed my chin. "You have no idea what you're talking about. And this is my house. I shouldn't have to lock doors."

I stuck out my lower lip and glared at him in defiance. "Your house until you decide to throw a party for half of Manhattan. Don't be angry with me just because you fucked up."

"Watch your tone with me, Raven. I'm still your boss." He walked me backward until I was up against the wall. With my wrist still in his grasp, he pinned it over my head.

My heart raced. His face was so close to mine and as much as I wanted to slap him, I also wanted to drown in his lips. "Fine, I'll keep your weird little secret, but don't you dare threaten me."

He smirked. "You're feisty tonight, Raven. I think this is the most fire I've ever seen from you. I like it. Relax, I'm not threatening you. I'm asking you nicely to please keep what you saw to yourself." He loosened his grip on my wrist and I snatched it down away from him.

"Tell me why you have them. Are you sick or something?" Maybe he needed transfusions?

Ozi looked away, his smile fading. "Not exactly. Depends on how you look at it, I guess. I can't tell you anything more. Not at this time."

"You don't trust me," I stammered, breathless.

"I don't trust anyone."

"Well, that's why you are alone." I couldn't tell if he was going to fly into a rage or burst out laughing.

He stepped forward again, pressing into me with his body, his hands against the wall, boxing me in. "I'm not alone right now."

There was something so wrong about this but I couldn't tear myself away. His brown eyes gazed into mine and my breath caught in my throat. He was so damn sexy. I never knew that men like him even existed—seductive, powerful, captivating.

"I should get back up with the wine before Enzo has a heart attack." I fixated on his lips. Hungered for them.

"You are right where you are supposed to be." Without warning, his lips crashed into mine.

I sucked in a breath at the contact, melting. If desire could be tasted, it would taste like him. I kissed him back, hard. Like it was the last kiss I was ever going to have. He squeezed my hips and I let out a whimper. His mouth was hot like fire and his tongue danced around mine, sending tingles down my legs.

I was getting lost, swept away. His kisses deepened as he wrapped his arms around my waist, locking me inside his embrace. I ran my fingers through his wavy hair, weaving them in and out. It was silky and smelled like roses and tobacco.

"I could take you right here in this room. On the cold cement floor," he whispered between kisses. "Or up against this wall...on the stairs...I want to bend you over that barrel and fuck you until your heart explodes."

And in the dark, damp cellar of blood and danger...I wanted to let him.

Thirteen

Ozi

HER BEAUTIFUL BROWN EYES WIDENED. HER PULSE quickened at my touch. I didn't have to slip my hands between her legs to know she was dripping wet. I could smell it on her. But she stiffened. Pulled away.

"I—I can't," Raven mumbled.

I backed away with a smirk. "Because I'm your boss? Fine, then I'll fire you."

Her eyelids fluttered up at me. "It's not just that… I'm not ready to be with another man yet."

"At some point, Raven, you are going to have to allow yourself to feel pleasure again." I brushed a fallen strand of hair out of her eyes and she quivered.

"I know," she whispered. "It's just hard…"

I started toward her again, but she fled. Her tiny frame bounced up the stairs without a glance back.

I waited a few minutes before leaving and locking the door behind me. I couldn't risk anyone else finding my stash and asking questions. I wasn't usually this careless, but with everything going on with Camille, the hacker, and Raven…I was highly distracted these days. I believed Raven would keep my secret but it wouldn't be long before she started asking more questions and I wasn't ready to answer them with the truth. Raven wasn't like the rest, but I thought that about Camille at one time too. I still wasn't sure I could trust her with my secrets. If I showed her who I really was and she rejected me…I don't think my heart could handle it.

When I finally joined Cassius on the terrace, I noticed something was wrong. Something in his expression. He was stiff, his face pained. I followed his gaze and my muscles twitched. "How did she get in here?"

Cassius shook his head. "How does Camille do anything? I haven't taken my eyes off her since I saw her."

The rage I felt was strong enough to wipe out an entire city. Not only did Camille crash my party, she had Raven cornered over by the caviar station. "I knew she was going to be trouble again. I need to get her away from Raven before she ruins everything."

"Just keep cool, brother. You don't want to cause a scene. That's what she's hoping for," Cassius muttered under his breath. "She loves to provoke you."

"Don't worry, I'll be a perfect gentleman." I winked and flashed my fangs before charging over to them.

I came up behind Camille and pinched her elbow, pulling her into my chest as I did. "A word please. Now. In the study," I whispered angrily into her ear. I turned toward Raven and gave a slight nod. "Pardon the interruption, Miss Deveraux and I have some business to discuss."

Camille eyed me like a cat who was readying to pounce. "By all means, lead the way. Raven, it's been a pleasure. I'm sure our paths will cross again."

At that, I yanked on her elbow and led her through the crowd. As we passed Cassius, he turned and followed.

Camille kept a plastered smile on her face even as she gritted her teeth. "Why is the wolf following us?"

Cassius always did make Camille nervous. He made most vampires nervous for that matter. Aside from the fact that he was the alpha of his pack, which meant he was deadlier than all of them put together, he also had silver on him at all times. Despite what the movies depicted, silver was deadly to vampires, not werewolves. I liked the fact that I had a werewolf as a best friend. It kept all the other creatures at bay.

"Just an insurance policy to make sure you stay in line," I spat at her.

I shoved her into the study while Cassius shut the door behind the three of us. "Start talking Camille. What are you doing here?"

She rested her ass against my desk and leaned back. "Don't mind if I make myself comfortable for your lecture now, do you?" No matter how much I despised her, she was still sexy as hell. Wearing a tight black dress with a plunging neckline, I couldn't help myself from admiring the shape of her. From her perfectly perky tits all the way down her slender calves to her red stilettos. It was a shame that all she had was venom running through her veins. I remember how sweet she first tasted.

"Answer the question. What are you doing in my house? *Again?*"

"So paranoid, Ozi. Relax, one of my investors invited me. I didn't know it was your house. I swear." She batted her fake eyelashes at me demurely, but I knew better. There was nothing demure about her.

Cassius feigned a cough. "Bullshit."

She glared at him; her eyes glowing. "Oh, sweet Cassius. Still bitter that I chose to fuck Ozi instead of you?" She giggled as his face turned beet red.

My patience was waning. "Enough. I don't care who invited you, you're not welcome here. You need to leave now. And stay away from my staff."

She scooted herself fully onto my desk and crossed her legs as she licked her red painted lips. "You mean, stay away from Raven, right? She must be special if you are being so protective over her. I was simply letting her know that there was more than one restaurant in New York to work at. That if she ever felt…uncomfortable, she had…options."

Before I could stop myself, I flew across the room and wrapped my hands around her neck. "How dare you. *Dolce Sale* and everyone in it, including Raven, belongs to me. I implicitly told you to stay away from what is mine."

Camille laughed and held my gaze. "She doesn't belong to you until you claim her. And you know what that entails. Until then, rules are rules. She's fair game. Maybe I'll claim her for myself." She winked and I lost it.

Cassius had to pry my hands off her neck. "Ozi, let her go."

I backed off and straightened my tie. "Get out."

She slithered off the desk like a snake. "I'll see myself out. Remember what I said." The sound of her heels clicking across the floor, the way she pranced off satisfied with herself, it was enough to send me over the edge.

Cassius shoved a whiskey in my hand. "She's just trying to get a rise out of you and it's clearly working. The angrier you get, the more she will fuck with Raven. You need to take it down a notch."

I shot the whiskey down and poured another. "She's right though. I have no claim to her."

"Have you thought about—"

"What? Making Raven a vampire?" I didn't need a mirror to know that my face was twisted in horror at the thought.

Cassius sighed. "Yes. If you want to be with her. If you…love her. Then that's the only way you can keep her safe."

He was right. Camille was right. Even Enzo was right about me staying away from her. But it was too late. I'd already painted a target on Raven's back the minute I took an interest in her. Camille wasn't stupid. She'd no doubt seen me fuck hundreds of girls that I simply discarded the next morning. She knew this one was different. And she was going to use it against me. This was payback. She was going to try to force me to turn Raven. Because if I didn't, Camille would find a way to turn her herself.

"I never wanted it to come to that. I'm going to ruin that girl's life. But what choice do I have now?"

Cassius nodded. "She might surprise you. Tell her the truth, Ozi. Tell her how you feel. She's not like Camille. Maybe she will embrace it."

I nearly choked on my drink. "Right. Because humans respond so well to supernatural phenomena. She'll probably try to drive a stake through my heart like they do in the movies."

"We both know that's not going to work. But you need to do something before Camille sinks her fangs into her."

"I know," I whispered.

Other than Enzo, I hadn't shown another human what I was in hundreds of years. The thought of it terrified me. The reaction. The fear mixed with horror that Camille gave me on the night that I turned her. The hatred in her eyes. It was more than I could bear. The heartbreak and pain sent me into a hundred year funk. I killed a lot in that century. And now it seemed history was repeating itself. Only this time, I hoped it wouldn't end in a bloodbath.

Raven

Something was up with Ozi and that blonde. I didn't know him that well but by the way he gripped her arm, it was easy to see he was furious with her. He tried to play it cool, but I saw right through it. He was not his normal charming self with her. There was something feral in his eyes when he looked at her. Not lust or love, but undeniable fury. I could only imagine what she had done to piss him off. He nearly tore my head off for discovering his blood bags.

Ugh the blood bags. I'd been racking my brain to figure out why he would be stockpiling them. He didn't seem sick. In fact, he was one of the healthiest looking people I'd ever seen. His skin glowed with a radiance that were usually only possible with a photo filter on social media. His body was lean and muscular. His hair thick and shiny. No, he didn't look sickly at all.

Maybe the blood bags were for a friend or family member? Or one of his housekeeping staff? Rich people could be bizarre and eccentric but this was weird even on that level.

I went into the kitchen with a tray full of plates and nearly dropped them when I heard my name. Then came the snickering and spiteful laughter. I paused outside the door to listen.

"Can you believe he defended her? They must be sleeping together," Tori murmured.

The other voice was Mara's, one of the on call servers who only came out for the parties.

"Wouldn't be the first time. She's just so not his usual type. She looks like she came straight from the farm."

"Well, we better be careful. Ozi made it clear he'd fire us if he catches us talking about Raven again." Tori lowered her voice.

Mara replied, "Wow. You've been with *Dolce Sale* for ten years. He'd fire you over some newbie? She must be good in bed."

They both erupted into quiet laughter, shushing each other like babbling teenagers. I'd heard enough. The nerve of these idiots to assume I was sleeping with the boss. But were they right? Did he favor me? There was something going on between us that I couldn't quite wrap my head around. We'd kissed twice now and we couldn't seem to stay away from each other. Maybe the girls were right to hate me. To be jealous of me. I didn't quite understand it myself. I'd seen a few of the women Ozi's been with. They were more sophisticated than me. Sexier than me. I didn't get why he wanted me.

I made a point to come in loudly, letting the plates bang around in the dish tub.

"Careful, Raven, you're going to break all of Ozi's plates," Tori snapped.

She ripped the tub out of my hands as she shook her head and rolled her eyes in annoyance.

"Sorry. This was the last of the dishes on the terrace. Anything else you need help with?" Exhaustion was setting in and all I wanted to do was take a hot shower and go to bed.

"Nope. We're done in here too. It's party time." Tori grinned at Mara.

Max ambled in. "Ladies, what's taking you so long? I already got the tequila shots lined up in the guest house. Music is pumping. Let's go, come on."

An overwhelming sense of dread came over me. Other than Max, these people hated me. And now they were turning our sleeping quarters into a party den. I could barely stand working with them. The last thing I wanted to do was lower my defenses and inhibitions by getting drunk with them. I needed to find another place to sleep tonight.

"Um, sorry, guys, I'm not up for partying. Is there another guest house I could just crash out in?" I was already an outsider with them. What did it matter if I isolated myself even more?

They all exchanged a look that seemed to say *I told you so.*

"Raven, you have to come. It's tradition," Max whined.

Tori chimed in, "Max, if she's too tired then let her be. There will be other parties. Right, Raven?"

She was only defending me because I was the last person she wanted to party with as well. "Thanks Tori," I replied flatly.

She squealed with delight despite Max giving her the sad eyes. "I'm sure Enzo can find you a quiet place to sleep tonight. Or maybe Ozi will."

Mara whipped around toward the sink to stifle a laugh while Max arched an eyebrow at me. I had never felt more uncomfortable in all of my life. Like I was some freakshow on display for them to gawk at. "Um, cool. I'll leave you all to it then. Have fun."

I bolted out of there before anyone could say another word. But I couldn't drown out the giggling that I'd left in my wake. It echoed off the marble floors behind me until I'd reached the foyer. I was about to burst into tears until I turned the corner and ran straight into Ozi. Literally.

Fourteen

Raven

OZI STOOD IN THE FOYER LOOKING DISHEVELED. HIS FACE WAS pained and sweaty. Like he had just run a marathon. He gazed at me mysteriously. Probably wondering why I wasn't in the guest house with the others. I wondered that myself. But I had enough of the gossip and excessive taunting.

"Hi. Do you know if there's a bus or taxi I can get out here? I'm going to head back to the city," I said.

His eyes widened. "Why? What happened? I have plenty of beds for you to sleep here."

I hesitated. I didn't want to be a snitch. The last thing I needed was to give Tori and her evil minions another reason to talk shit about me. "I'm just tired and I don't feel like partying. I need a quiet place to lay down. Honestly, if it's not too much trouble, I'd rather just head back to my place."

Ozi contemplated what I said. His face ranged from a flash of emotions that I couldn't quite place. But it seemed to only add to his stress and exhaustion. "Raven, I don't know what happened and it's fine if you don't want to talk about it, but the city is three hours away. I would offer my helicopter but it's already one AM and my pilot is probably asleep. Look, I have plenty of space here. I'll see to it you get a quiet room upstairs where you won't be disturbed... Please stay."

I really didn't want to trek three hours back to the city and his house was more than comfortable. But being in such close proximity to Ozi was nerve wrecking. All I wanted to do when I looked at him was tear his clothes off. I didn't want to be *that* girl. The one Tori and Mara were convinced I was. But there was a spark between us that was getting harder and harder to resist.

"I just need to sleep. That's it."

He smiled. "If you are worried about having a repeat of our little kiss downstairs, don't. I will not force the issue if it makes you uncomfortable. You have my word that no one will bother you tonight. Especially me."

I was a bit disappointed that he gave up so soon. Even though that's basically what I've been asking him to do. *Ugh. What was wrong with me?*

"Okay. I'll stay. Thank you."

His eyes lit up. "Perfect. Follow me. I'll show you to your room."

I followed Ozi up the spiral staircase that led to a lavish upstairs level. The floors were marble and the windows were dressed in red velvet drapes. The décor was Southern Gothic meets Italian Renaissance. The halls revealed rows upon rows of doors, much like the downstairs wine cellar. Again, I wondered why a man living by himself would need so many rooms?

We stopped at a door that was nestled in an alcove. "Here you are, Raven. Let me know if you need anything. There's a call button next to the bed that rings directly to my staff. They will bring you anything you want at any time. And if you have any questions or concerns, I'm just the third door down on the left...There's also a lock on the door if it makes you feel better."

He must have seen the apprehension on my face. "Oh, I don't think that will be necessary but thank you for letting me know." I didn't want him to think I was afraid of him. As persistent as he's been, he's also been a gentleman.

"All right then, goodnight, Raven." He bent down and placed a light peck on my forehead.

Every cell in my body awakened. Just the slightest touch from his soft lips sent my senses into overdrive. What kind of magic did he possess that he could just get under my skin like that?

"Goodnight, Ozi." I went in and shut the door before I was tempted to make out with him again.

The bedroom mirrored something out of an expensive European hotel. "Oh wow," I said under my breath.

The four poster bed was wrapped in gold threaded netting, encasing a king size bed fitted with silk sheets and fluffy pillows. The windows were dressed in black velvet drapes, tied back with gold ropes. It was almost too pretty to mess up. Like something you'd see in a museum or magazine.

An open walk-in closet revealed clothing and shoes conveniently in my size. *That's odd.* Inside was an antique dresser. I opened up the drawers and found an array of silk pajamas, lacey lingerie, and even yoga pants. I opted for a silk chemise tank and matching pajama shorts. Ozi had done too good a job of heating my room and I didn't want to sweat all over his silk sheets. I was already hot and bothered knowing he was just down the hall.

Ugh, there I go again. Why did my brain always wander to sex with him? When I was with Alex, I loved our intimate moments but it wasn't quite so carnal. I didn't crave Alex's touch the way I did Ozi's. I had never craved anyone's touch the way I do his.

I drank the glass of water that someone had set on the dresser and then climbed into the silky sheets. As soon as I laid my head down, I was instantly relaxed. My sore muscles began to finally unclench and sink into the floaty marshmallow bed.

But I couldn't sleep. My mind and body were both wide awake despite how tired I thought I'd felt earlier. I was finally in bed in a quiet room, but all I could think about was Ozi. How his hands would feel on my body. How his lips tasted earlier when he found me in the room I wasn't supposed to be in. How dangerous it felt. The way I enraged him yet excited him at the same time. A tingle rolled down my thighs and I was lightly damp.

I threw the sheets back and stared up at the canopy for a few minutes before doing what I swore I told myself I wasn't going to do. I peeked out into the hall and seeing it empty, tiptoed toward his room.

Ozi opened the door after one knock. I didn't know what I was going to say or what I was even doing here in the middle of the night. I just needed to see him again. I craved his presence like a drug.

A smirk edged at the corners of his mouth. "You looking for something?"

"I—I don't know," I stammered.

He leaned into the door frame, towering over me with nothing on except black trousers. His tanned chest was ripped and covered in black and gray tattoos.

"What can I do for you, Raven?" He lowered his head toward mine until I could feel his hot breath on my face. What in the hell *was* I doing? This was dangerous.

"Thank you for sticking up for me earlier. I overheard Tori and Mara talking." I looked down but he lifted my chin up so I'd have to look him in the eyes.

"You have such a beautiful soul, Raven. So kind and caring. When I see anyone trying to hurt you…it brings out a side of me that I didn't know I had. I want to protect you, darling."

No one had ever protected me before. I'd always been so alone. Tears threatened to spill out at the thought of it. "I…I shouldn't be here. Sorry. Have a good night." I backed into the hallway, suddenly aware of how vulnerable I was and how little I was wearing. My nipples poked through the thin cotton fabric of my tank top like high beams.

"Yes, you should." In one quick motion, he pulled me into his room, shut the door, and pinned me up against it. His hands pressed into my wrists which he held firm above my head. My body quivered, ached for him. I couldn't take it anymore. His lips traced the tip of my ear and he inhaled a deep breath. "Tell me to stop, and I will," he whispered. "Just say the word."

I couldn't. I didn't want him to. He held both my wrists with one strong hand while his other trailed down my chest, stopping short at the neckline of my tank top. His fingers teased, dipping just below the edge. He stroked the line of the fabric while just barely caressing my skin.

I was practically panting as our eyes never broke contact. I had never been this turned on before ever. I wanted more. "Please...don't stop," I murmured.

The look in his eyes turned feral, hungry. His hands trembled and his muscles tightened as if he were holding back. He was doing everything he could to restrain himself. His lips inched closer to mine and hovered just slightly out of reach. He was teasing me. Making me ache for it. He pulled one side of my tank top down, exposing my breast. I let out a gasp as he squeezed my nipple between his fingers. His pressure increased as I arched my back up and pressed my cheek into the door.

He pulled down the other side and did the same, squeezing my nipple so hard and then releasing it, stroking it lightly in slow circles. It was driving me crazy. I twisted back and forth but his one hand still held my wrists firmly in place above my head.

Ozi gently wrapped his hand around my neck and crushed his lips onto mine. And I lost it. His tongue plunged into my mouth, carnal and vicious, hungrily exploring, almost bruising my lips in his urgency. And then he slowed, twirling the tip of his tongue around mine.

"Do you want to feel true pleasure?" He kissed my neck as he whispered. "Do you want me to give it to you?"

"*Yes…*" I murmured.

He dragged his tongue across my collarbone and my whole body shivered. "Have you ever been tied up before, Raven?"

I hadn't, but the thought of it stimulated every nerve in my body. I would let him do whatever he wanted to me right now. I swallowed hard. "No…"

"Do you want me to?" His fingers were back to tracing circles around my nipples. I could barely think, let alone stand any longer.

"Yes," I whispered. I needed to feel something other than heartache for once. I needed to feel alive.

He released my wrists. "Lay on the bed."

My knees wobbled as I stumbled over to the bed. Black silk sheets welcomed me. I climbed up and laid back as he said, quivering in anticipation.

He watched me, his gaze traveling over every inch of my body. He climbed onto the bed next to me and reached for my wrists again. Above my head was a black leather rope with two loops. It hung from the ceiling. Ozi slipped my wrists through and tightened it so I couldn't break free. He yanked my hips, sliding me down and the rope moved with me. For a split second I was terrified and strangely excited at the same time. I wasn't going anywhere and I was at his mercy.

Ozi stroked my cheek. "If you want to be released at any point, say so and I will untie you instantly. I only want to bring you pleasure."

He was a man of many faces—gentle and kind as well as dangerous and wild. I gave him a nod and held my breath as he slowly tore the chemise tank down the middle, exposing my breasts.

"I'll buy you another one." He cupped my breasts, rubbing my nipples in between his fingers.

I arched toward the ceiling. "Don't stop."

He squeezed harder then dragged his fingers down my ribs, across my hips and stomach, then rested them just below my belly button.

I held his gaze as he gently pulled my shorts and panties off at the same time.

"Part your legs for me, darling." He stroked the inside of my right thigh, urging me to spread apart for him.

I didn't know how much more I could take. The waiting, the buildup to what was going to be the most insane climax I've ever felt. I opened my legs a little, unsure of what he wanted.

"Wider, darling," he moaned in my ear. "I want to see all of you."

I spread out like a butterfly, so wide the backs of my thighs pressed into the bed. "How's this?" I murmured. My heart was racing. All I wanted was him inside me.

He parted the flesh between my legs, rubbing and caressing in slow strokes. I let out a whimper as his fingers caressed the outer flesh, teasing me. "Fuck...you are so wet."

"Yes," I panted. "I want more." I could barely speak through bated breath. If my hands hadn't been restrained, I would have pushed his hand farther.

I arched my hips up and he plunged his finger inside. I cried out and clenched around him.

He moaned. "And so tight too..."

I twisted and jerked with every thrust of his hand, aching for more. He sucked on my breasts, drawing circles around my nipples with his tongue. I thought I was going to explode.

I had never wanted anyone so badly before. Ozi had me completely in his control and it was everything I needed.

"Do you want me, Raven?" His voice was raspy.

"Ye—yes...*please*, Ozi." I could barely get the words out my heart was beating so fast.

He moved to the end of the bed and removed his silk trousers. He stood over me, gazing down with a devilish smirk. "I told you I would have you. I'm a man of my word."

Fifteen

Ozi

I HAD HER RIGHT WHERE I WANTED HER. *UNDERNEATH ME.*
She looked like an angel. Her skin glistened, glowing like an ethereal goddess who had just tied her very existence to mine. There were no words to describe the magnetic pull I had to her. *Why Raven?* She was pure, innocent, yet raw and wild. She carried pain same as me and I wanted to take it away. And she was the most beautiful thing I'd ever seen.

I untied her wrists and lowered myself onto her. She tightened around me, gasping with pleasure as I entered her slowly. The sensation was overwhelming and I had to fight every urge to sink my teeth into her neck. I didn't want to hurt her but I wanted to consume every part of her. To taste her blood. Her juices. Everything.

She moaned as I slid in and out. Each thrust became more powerful than the last as I rushed to fill her. She squirmed with pleasure, biting down on my shoulder in such a way that I could not with her. She wanted to taste me just as bad and it drove me crazy. Her legs opened wider as she clawed at my back, urging me deeper inside.

We rocked against each other like it was the last time any two people would ever smash their bodies into each other. It was the most explosive rush I'd ever felt. I grabbed a fist full of her hair as she arched her back, bringing her up from the bed so she could straddle me in my lap.

I pulled her legs around my waist and crashed into her again. I guided her hips up and down as she threw her head back, crying out loud enough to wake the whole house. There was no stopping. No slowing down. Her hard nipples rubbed against my chest as I dug my fingers deeper into her thighs.

Her chin tilted toward me and I covered her lips with mine. The sweet and salty taste of her tongue drove me wild. "You're mine," I whispered.

This made her moan louder. She gazed at me with longing, aching, and desire. "Yes," she whispered back. "I'm yours…"

I flipped her on her back and plunged into her so deep, I thought my dick was going to explode. The blood rushed to the tip and I couldn't hold it back any longer. I cried out as the orgasm took over all my limbs. My muscles tensed and twitched. I collapsed on top of her as I came. She trembled against me, panting and gasping, her legs quivering. She wrapped her arms around my neck and clung to me like I was an anchor in her ocean.

My mind was made up.

I was never going to let her go.

Raven

Ozi's chest heaved underneath my cheek. I had never experienced an orgasm like that ever. My entire body sang like a bird. I was addicted now. How could I ever be with somebody else after that? Ozi owned that part of me now. I didn't even know what that meant or how we would navigate this, but I wanted more. I wanted him again and again. Lust was a powerful force. Maybe even more powerful than love. All I knew, was that I was at his mercy and I never wanted to be free of him.

"Are you okay?" he asked.

"I wasn't expecting that. When I came to your door…I don't know what I was thinking. I mean, I did know what I was thinking. I guess what I'm trying to say is that I didn't come out here with the intentions of showing up at your room in the middle of the night…but I'm glad I did."

He chuckled and pulled my arm tight across his chest, stroking it back and forth. "I knew you wouldn't be able to resist me for much longer. I'm happy you came too. In more ways than one."

I giggled. "Multiple times."

His breathing began to steady. "Raven…there are things about me that may make you change your mind. Things that might make you want to run away."

"We all have a past, Ozi. I have my demons too." I was starting to think that he actually might care about me beyond just the sex.

He pulled away and sat up, gazing down at me with his haunting brown eyes. "That's what I'm talking about. I don't have demons. Raven…I am the demon."

I shuddered as soon as he said it. "What do you mean?"

He got out of bed and pulled on his pants. "I don't want to scare you away. Not when I've only just found you. There are things I will tell you in time. But just know that no matter what happens, I will never hurt you. Just promise me, you'll keep an open mind."

He wasn't making any sense. I definitely got the dramatic vibe from him, but the way he was talking was bizarre. "Look, I want to get to know you better. In just one night, you've made me feel more alive than I have in years. I feel safe with you, so…stop calling yourself a demon."

Ozi went to the window and pulled back the velvet drapes. The moonlight shining on his face only highlighted the shadows in his eyes. "In time, you will learn things about me. Things you might not like. But I'm not the same as I once was."

"Ozi, I am the last person who would judge you for your past. I have things I'm not proud of either. I get it…I'm afraid too. If you are having second thoughts about me—"

"No. Never." He rushed to my side and cupped my face in his hands. "It is you that may have regrets someday. In my long existence, I have never been more sure. If I were a selfless man, I'd order you to leave right now. But I'm none of those things."

And yet I couldn't make myself get up and leave. I wanted to stay in this room forever with him. What had gotten into me? I wasn't my-self. Maybe he was just being over dramatic with poetic metaphors. "Ozi, you don't have to hide who you are with me. You'll see."

He picked me up and lifted me onto the floor. I backed up as he pressed me into the wall. His lips hovered over mine as his eyes searched my face. "Raven, I'm not a typical man. This won't be a typical relationship. You are free to walk away whenever you choose. Can you handle that?"

"And what is a typical relationship? The kind where the one you love cheats on you? I am done with typical. I want different. I'm not going anywhere." I held his gaze.

He let out an exasperated sigh and pulled me to his bare chest, cupping the back of my head in his hands. "We will take this as slow or as fast as you want. I am not good at relationships but for you I want to try."

I was still unsure as to why he was being so cryptic. What could he possibly tell me about himself that would make me want to run? I wasn't so naïve to guess that he probably had a troubled past. He was a powerful billionaire and status like that didn't come without a price. But no matter what he did or didn't do, one thing I was certain of. The one thing that I felt in my bones without any rational explanation was that I had to play this out. Even if it ended. It would be worth it just to feel this way again.

"I know you have the next few days off. Stay here for the weekend. We can talk, eat, drink…fuck some more. I'll have whatever you need sent over." His eyes pleaded with me.

I had just promised him I would try to open up, to get to know him, so I couldn't run off now. I hadn't felt this vulnerable since I left Maplewood with my heart shattered into a million pieces. "Okay. I can do that."

His face lit up. "*Belissimo*. Now, let's get back into bed." He winked and my stomach flipped. The twinkle in his eye was the only indication I needed to let me know that I wasn't going to get any sleep and he was going to make me come all night.

Raven

I stifled a yawn and rolled over to find the space next to me empty.

Sitting up, I saw he had laid out an outfit for me on the bed— skinny jeans, a yellow cashmere sweater similar to the one I wore when I ran into him at the Met, and a pair of black leather riding boots.

A note sat on top.

Buongiorno, darling, take as long as you like to shower and change. I'll be waiting for you on the terrace. Yours, Ozi.

I could feel a smile pulling at my lips. I'd never been pampered like this before. Alex's idea of romance was letting me pick the movie after I had cooked and done all the dishes. It was our fifth anniversary and he showed up at my house with a six pack of beer, smelling like he had already downed a few. We ordered pizza and fell asleep watching some sports channel.

Back home, that's how all the guys were. They worked all day and drank beer all night. Date night was going to the Maplewood tavern for shitty hamburgers and cheap wine. I thought that was normal back then. Actually, I thought that was normal until about a week ago when Ozi took me to Juliet's. Not that I didn't still love a good greasy burger, but not every single night. That got old real fast.

I showered in the lavish bathroom. The counter was stocked with beautiful and exquisite smelling soaps and lotions. I dressed in the outfit he'd laid out for me and made my way downstairs. The house was even more gorgeous with the sunlight shining in. I could see all of the wood and marble sparkling with fresh eyes. I stepped out onto the terrace and couldn't hide the awe on my face.

My mouth dropped open. Ozi sat waiting for me at a table covered in treats—waffles, blueberry pancakes, bacon, eggs, fruit, muffins, and pastries. A white gloved attendant stood nearby, holding a tray of mimosas.

"Ozi...this is too much. How can I possibly eat all of this?" My eyes were bigger than my stomach but not that big.

He shot me a playful grin and I lost my breath. His hair was still ruffled from our romp. He too wore a cashmere sweater, beige with a couple buttons at the neck that were undone. He looked like a catalog model. "Eat as much as your belly will take and I'll have the rest dropped off at the nearby food bank."

Oh, and he was a philanthropist too? Could this man be any more perfect? How could a demon, as he called himself, have such a big heart?

Sixteen

Raven

THE GROUNDS WERE BEAUTIFUL IN THE DAYLIGHT. AFTER stuffing my face with as many delectable pastries as I could muster, we went for a walk on his property. Emerald green grass sprawled out around us as we walked. The scent of it being freshly cut wafted in my nose, making me nostalgic for my youth. Summers in Maplewood were the best part of my childhood. Playing with the neighborhood kids down by the river and then racing back home as the sound of the ice cream truck called to us like a dinner bell.

Those were simpler times. Days when Alex and I were just innocents, falling into our puppy love without a care of the world around us. A slight ache in my heart resurfaced at the memory. A twinge of sadness and regret. Like being homesick for a person.

"Care to talk about it?" Ozi asked. I was so lost in my thoughts, I hadn't noticed he'd been studying me.

I shrugged. "Not much to tell. The truth is, I caught my boyfriend with another woman. My sister to be exact." I took a big swig of the champagne flute I'd brought with me for our walk.

Ozi's eyes softened. "You walked in on them? Oh, Raven. I'm so sorry."

"Yeah, I can't ever *unsee* that. Remember the night I ran out of the Red Apothecary? Well, I had just gotten a voicemail from him—Alex—telling me they're getting married."

Ozi took my hand in his. It felt soft and warm and strong. His fingers gently curled around mine, sending shivers up my spine. "I'm sorry, Raven. You deserve so much more than that. Men can be cruel and selfish. I hope I can show you different."

I was letting my mind wander back to a time that no longer existed when I was currently having a magical moment right now. "The past is the past. Tell me about you. How did you end up here? When did you leave Italy?"

He pulled me over to a shaded spot under a great oak tree. His smile became almost dreamlike. "I came over on a boat in…" He hesitated, sighed, and then continued. "It was a very long time ago. I left Italy to explore the world. I wanted adventure. The boat took me here to New York. I made my way down to New Orleans where some of my cousins were. I fell in love with…all of it—the women, the music, the booze. That's where I met Cassius and Lux. We went into business together and ended up back in New York some years ago. Not too exciting." He winked.

"Were you always in the restaurant business? Forgive me if this is rude, but I can't imagine you making billions of dollars on just a couple of restaurants and one winery."

He leaned against the tree and crossed his arms casually. "No. You are correct. We have other ventures. And I don't think you are rude in the slightest. I think you are beautiful and sexy." His gaze flickered with mischief and fire. It stirred a tingly sensation in my belly and all the way down between my thighs.

It also made me nervous. He was being open but holding back. I could hear it in his voice. There were things he was leaving out. Sugar coating a story that was most likely steeped in danger and intrigue. He didn't trust many people.

"How many women have you…." I couldn't finish.

"Have I fucked?" A smirk turned up the corners of his lips.

"Have you brought here? To your house?" There was no doubt in my mind that he'd slept with half of New York but how many women he'd gotten close to was a mystery.

Ozi ambled toward me in a slow sexy swagger. "I have had a few but never in the main house. And never overnight. You are the first, Raven. I don't know why you're different, but you just are." He towered over me, taking my face between his hands. My heart raced. His full lips moistened as he stroked a finger down the side of my cheek. "Maybe it's because you don't want anything from me."

I swallowed hard as the space between us was closing. "I don't know what I want most of the time," I murmured. His fingers locked behind my neck and then crept down my spine as he began lightly kneading them into my shoulder blades. "I think I want…you. Nothing from you. Just to be with you."

Desire flashed in his eyes and he tugged me closer. His lips smashed down on mine, wet and hungry. I whimpered slightly as his tongue explored mine, like a waltz. The taste of salt and maple syrup filled my mouth. I kissed him back with a passion matching his own. I couldn't get enough. I wanted more of his flesh.

Last night he took control, but now it was my turn. I didn't know what was coming over me or who this new person was that I was turning into but it felt amazing. Maybe this was who I was always meant to be and I just needed Ozi to show me.

I came up for air and stepped back. He licked his lips as he admired me. Without any worry or fear who might be watching, I pulled my sweater up over my head and then removed my bra. I let out a sweet shudder as the wind tickled my breasts.

Ozi sat down on the grass and leaned back against his elbows. "Take off the rest."

Ozi

The stiff muscle between my legs throbbed at the sight of her bare breasts. The way the slightest breeze hardened her nipples. With the sun shining behind her and her dark wavy hair cascading around her naked flesh, she looked like a goddess.

Raven slid out of her jeans and panties. And for fuck's sake, I almost came right there. She was a vision. She trembled with nerves but the fierce look in her eyes told me she was determined to perform for me. I eased back on the grass and waited for her command.

She stood over me, strong and beautiful, then lowered herself down to the grass beside me. She pressed me down flat and began unbuttoning my shirt, pleased with what she was seeing. This woman was going to be the death of me. Every touch led to a shiver. I wanted to consume her with an appetite that was insatiable. Even just her scent threatened to send me over the edge. I had to fight with every ounce of strength in my soul to not take her against that tree. I wanted her to think she was in control. She needed to feel what that was like. If she was going to be my mate, I needed her to be powerful.

Her trembling fingers undid the button on my slacks, sliding the zipper down slow. I moaned with anticipation. Once she had my pants off, she climbed on top of me and rubbed her breasts against my chest. The sensation was electric. Her kisses were soft and slow, moving down my chest. The wet tip of her tongue danced across my abs and my muscles twitched.

I was at her mercy and I loved it. Giving up control was a new type of delicious torture. Her eyes held me in place, as they never left my gaze, locked in a fiery stare down that filled my soul with more desire than I had ever felt.

"I want to be inside you, Raven. *Please...*" It was more than I could take.

A devilish grin spread across her face as she mounted me. I gasped at the shift. With her tiny hands she grabbed my dick and inched it inside her.

"Fuck..." She was so tight and wet. My blood raced forward, pushing me to the brink. I held her hips still. Or else I was going to explode inside her before we even began.

She teased her fingernails down my chest. "Does that feel good?" she asked innocently, but she knew exactly what she was doing and already knew the answer.

My carnal instincts took over and the animal inside me kicked in. I flipped her over and smashed into her. Her body arched up as she moaned in delight. Her insides were like an inferno. Like a fiery ocean. With every thrust the spark between us grew, crackling like electricity. Our limbs and lips entangled in a frenzy. Blades of grass and dirt covered us, sticking to our skin underneath the hot sun.

"Harder," she whispered.

I growled into her ear, pressing my nose against her cheek so I could breathe her into my very bones. I pounded harder, faster, pushing her into the ground like a snow angel. The vein in her neck throbbed. I sucked on the flesh that covered it. Parting my lips around it, the tips of my fangs stretched out. I wanted to taste beneath the flesh. Her sweat and salt and blood. All of her.

She moaned and writhed underneath me. She clawed at my back, pulled at my hair, and squeezed her thighs around my ass, digging her heels into the backs of legs, urging me deeper. And the vein in her neck pulsed, beckoning me. Seducing me. I had to be careful but I could play a little.

I gently took her flesh between my teeth, nibbling in delicate strokes but careful to not break the skin. I knew what it would happen if I did. One drop of her blood in my mouth and it would be over. The lightness of my teeth on her neck sent her into overdrive. She thrusted her hips up hard and arched her neck back, pressing my head to her vein. "Don't stop," she begged.

But I had to.

Or I would not be able to ever stop until I drank every drop.

I forced my lips away from her neck and smashed them down hard against her lips.

She squeezed her pussy tight around my dick and cried out. I had her right where I wanted her. The blood raced to the tip of my dick and tingled. I dug my fingers into her hips and tugged them up as I pounded deeper into her. I couldn't hold back anymore. I grunted then yelled out as a final shiver shot through. At the same time, she held her breath and trembled against me as we exploded all over each other.

We laid in the cool grass, our legs still intertwined. I rested my hand on her thigh. "Fuck, Raven…" I could barely speak let alone breathe. My body was still orgasming and twitching as wave after wave of pleasure rippled through me.

She let out a deep breath. "You've ruined me for anyone else."

My heart skipped a beat. I knew what she meant and I got a strange satisfaction from it. We came over and over again—in the grass, under the oak tree, until the sun began to set and the stars stole the sky like an army of fireflies. The more time I spent around Raven, the more that feeling of being lost and broken began to fade away. It was like she was plucking the pain out of me, one kiss at a time. There were so many things I didn't know about her and that voice in my head whispered dangerous things. But I ignored the voice. I rolled over onto my side and pulled her face toward mine. "There will never be anyone else. You're mine now."

Her eyes flickered with something I'd never seen in her before. A wild, feral look of hunger and desire. A look that seemed to be buried under all that innocence and brokenness. She yanked me toward her with a strength I was not expecting. "Again," she whispered. "Fuck me again."

Seventeen

Ozi

My phone was blowing up with messages—Enzo, Charlie, and Cassius. I ducked into the study while Raven took a tour of the library. S he loved books, so as soon as I mentioned that I had a first edition of *Bram Stoker's Dracula*, she insisted on seeing it immediately. A vampire who collected fictional books about vampires… The irony was not lost on me.

The first message was from Charlie, wanting to know if I was interested in *any party favors*. The usual—women and booze. It had been over a week since I'd reached out to him so he was probably wondering where I was.

Then there were messages from Enzo. He noticed that Raven didn't get in the van with the other staff members and warned me again not to fuck things up for her.

And lastly, Cassius. Wanting to hang out and discuss business. Namely, the hacker situation.

I ignored all of them.

It had been decades since I was able to just relax and not worry about anything. Having Raven here in my home made me happier than I thought it would. The only thing gnawing at me was the elephant in the room. The giant, blood sucking elephant that she didn't even know existed. The last time I told a woman I loved what I really was, I ended up with Camille. And now that was coming back to haunt me.

I wanted to believe Raven was different, but you can never really know someone. Did I want to take that risk again? I couldn't hide it from her forever. At some point she was going to wonder why I disappeared every few hours into the cellar. She would start to question why I never got sick or injured or looked any older.

I turned off my phone and headed upstairs to the library. Raven was nestled on the couch, feet tucked underneath her, and engrossed in one of my books.

"The Count of Monte Cristo. Good choice. One of my favorites." I leaned against the doorway, admiring the serene look on her face as she read.

She peered up. "I've loved this story since I was a kid. It always made me wonder who people really were. Not the story they tell, but the true identity of every soul. I think we all hide those parts of ourselves."

I smiled. We were more alike than I'd thought. It was as if she understood what I was on some cellular level, even without knowing on a conscious one. "Some things must be hidden in order to protect oneself. Secrets are just that for a reason. Sometimes the reasons are valid ones. Tell me, Raven, do you have secrets?"

She gazed out the French windows, clutching the book to her chest. "Of course I do. But I think those around me have greater ones. My whole life I could feel it. That something wasn't right. The way everyone tiptoed around me waiting for the other shoe to drop. It was like they were all in on it except me. And so I never felt like I really belonged there. Not in Maplewood, not even in my own home."

A twinge of guilt rippled through me at the realization that I was one of those people in her life now that was keeping secrets from her. "The truth finds its way out eventually. Even when you don't want it to."

I knew that all too well.

She nodded and smiled lazily at me. "I know it's coming. And when whatever it is does, I know that there will be no going back. Everything will change."

I wanted to shield her from all of it. Protect her forever. But there was no avoiding this destiny. Not unless I let her go. And I had no intention of doing so. I waited too long for someone like Raven. I just needed to find the right words and the right time before it was too late.

Raven

For the next two nights, Ozi and I were inseparable. It was like a dream. One that I didn't want to wake up from. For the first time in a long time, I didn't hurt. I didn't think about Alex or my family back home. I was just able to be present in the moment and feel things I never thought I'd feel again.

Ozi touched me in ways that I knew my body would always crave. As if all my cells were waking up from a long dreamless sleep. He was both rough and gentle at the same time. He brought out a side of me, a carnal side, that surprised me more than him. It was the weekend of endless orgasms and decadent indulgences. When he wasn't making me come, he was filling me up with five star delicacies and expensive champagne.

The most surprising revelation was how easy he was to talk to. That we actually had things in common. We both loved the same books and art. We could talk for hours about history and I loved that he knew a little bit about everything. Our conversations flowed easily. It was refreshing to be with a man who wasn't glued to the TV.

But there was something between us that wasn't right. It wasn't like the normal way people fall in love. We were consumed by each other. Consumed by lust. It was becoming an obsession. The more we touched, the more we wanted. My body was in a constant state of tremors and tingles. Just the slightest stroke of his fingertips across my belly sent me into a frenzy. This thing between us...it was like a drug. It was intoxicating.

He could make me fall. He could crush my heart into dust. And as much as that tiny voice in my head was screaming at me to run, I couldn't turn away. I wasn't the same since I'd first laid eyes on him. And now, even more, I knew that I couldn't go back to how I was before.

It was almost time to head back into the city and a deep aching dread tugged at my mind. My stomach was in knots. How was this going to work? What exactly were we to each other? He'd claimed my body but made no attempt to offer me his heart. Were two broken people even capable of love? Would this attraction and lust wear off, and if so, what then? Who would I be after?

Ozi hugged me tight to his chest under the covers. He caressed my shoulder with just the tips of his fingers, sending tiny shivers down my spine. "I've arranged a car to take you back home. I have some business to attend to for the next couple of days but then...I'd like to see you again."

Reality was crashing back in. I'd have to go back home to my empty apartment. Back to my job at his restaurant where most of the staff couldn't stand me. After this weekend, I could only imagine the gossip that would be floating around. Everyone knew I'd stayed behind to be with Ozi.

I traced circles on his chest with my fingers, enjoying the smoothness of it. "Ozi...I don't want things to be awkward between us at the restaurant. If you don't want me to work for you anymore, I'd understand. Sleeping with the boss was not my intention. I don't want anyone making you feeling uncomfortable about it."

He turned his head and placed a light kiss on my cheek. "You'll do nothing of the sort. You can work at *Dolce Sale* for as long as you like. Don't listen to them, Raven. You are not just some one night stand if that's what you're wondering. There are promises I'm not ready to make just yet. Secrets I'm not ready to share. But please be patient with me. I meant what I said…I'm never letting you go."

It was a strange thing to say considering we had no idea what we really meant to each other. How long could we hold onto this if we weren't willing to give ourselves over completely?

"Whatever you say, boss," I teased. I didn't know what else to say. As close as I felt to him right now, lying in his arms, I also felt this enormous distance and space. And there was always the part of me that believed that all men were like Alex. That one day, Ozi would grow tired of me, and leave me for someone else. Isn't that what men did? Most never seemed satisfied with what they had. Even my own father reeked of perfume most nights after staying late at the office. My mom looked the other way but the hurt in her eyes was too obvious to ignore. She settled because it was easier to patch up the boat than to rock it. I was too scared to get in the boat at all.

Ozi played with my hair, twirling strands through his fingers. "Where did you go, darling?"

"What do you mean? I'm right here."

He pressed a finger to my temple. "In your head. Where did you go in your head? I can hear it in your breath, in your heartbeat, you wandered off to somewhere else."

"I can't help it sometimes. Sorry. I've been trying to stay present. There are things that are hard to forget. Dark corners that I've become so used to, they don't even scare me anymore."

He shuddered and tightened his grip around my shoulders. "I'll protect you from the nightmares."

I felt warm and safe in his arms, but as I drifted off to sleep, I couldn't help but remember his words. *I don't have any demons. I am the demon.*

I didn't have any nightmares, or dreams for that matter, for the rest of the night. By morning, the sun was shining again and all of my fears felt silly. That was until he kissed me goodbye and put me in a car back to the city. The further the car took me away from his house, the bigger the ache in my chest became. Was it his absence? Suppressed emotions that were now resurfacing because I didn't have Ozi to distract me? It was a feeling like homesickness, only I wasn't sure which home I was missing more.

Two days. That's how long he said we'd be apart. I felt like the bubble was going to burst. But what could possibly change in two days?

Ozi

"Cassius. Did you find out anything?"

"A little but mostly firewalls. I need access to the local stuff. Feel like taking a trip?"

"Fuck. All right. I'll pick you up in an hour."

I hung up the phone and pulled up my GPS. It was a three hour drive to Maplewood. If we left soon, we could be back in New York by early morning tomorrow. We could drive all night. And we would if it meant getting some answers. There were things that just didn't add up. Things her family was keeping from her. And what were the odds that the hacker pinged activity from the same place that Raven grew up in? What were the odds that a girl from a small town interned at my winery in Italy and then coincidentally found herself working at my restaurant in New York? I needed to know if there was a connection.

This need to protect her grew stronger by the minute. I would tell her whatever I found out after but I didn't want to worry her for nothing. I placed a cooler full of blood bags in the back seat of my sedan and headed out to the lake to pick up Cassius. Even though it was still three more days till the next full moon, I'd also loaded the chains in the trunk just in case. There was a time when I was strong enough to hold him down with my bare hands, but with every shift, he became harder and harder to control. If he would just stop fucking about and find himself a mate, it wouldn't be as bad.

Back on the road with no driver, it was just me and Cassius on another adventure like the old days. If Lux were here, he'd call me an asshole but come along just so he could taunt me the whole way. He had a knack for talking shit but that was his way of showing love. We were brothers in a sense, the three of us. We'd do anything for each other. I didn't know what we were going to find in Maplewood. But something told me it was not going to be good.

Eighteen

Raven

I FIXATED ON THE GREEN OLIVES SWIRLING AROUND IN MY MARTINI glass, watching them float amidst the tiny ice crystals inside the vodka.

"Raven, you haven't said a word since we got here. What is going on with you, girl?" Max asked.

I shook my head and took a sip of my drink. "It's nothing. Sorry I missed brunch on Sunday. Something came up."

"It's fine. That's why they invented happy hour. And by something, you mean our deliciously fine boss, right?"

"No! I was organizing my closet." I couldn't look Max in the eye.

"For two days? Girl, please, everyone knows you didn't get on any of the vans on Sunday. So what happened?" He smirked as if he had just uncovered the secret to life.

The gossip mill was already churning so I thought I might as well tell him. I had to confide in someone. "We…hung out."

"You fucked him, didn't you?"

I could feel my cheeks burning. "Um...well. Yes."

Max let out a whoop and I grabbed his hands, pulling him in to shoosh him. "*Be quiet, Max.*"

He leaned back in his chair, satisfied that he got it out of me. "So how was it? Is he hung like a horse? I bet he's a good kisser. *Is he?* Tell me everything."

I downed the rest of my martini and signaled to the bartender for another. "Whoa, relax. I don't even have a good buzz yet."

He gave me a look, arching his eyebrow and tapping his fingers impatiently against the marble surface of the bar. "Spill the tea, Raven."

I cleared my throat as if that were supposed to help the words come out any easier and with less embarrassment. I wasn't a prude, but I had never had sex like that before in my life. Sex that would make any woman blush.

"It was amazing. Perfect," I stated as Max threw me another '*oh, you gotta do better than that*' look. "Okay it was fucking hot. He was good at everything. I've never been touched like that before."

Max's eyes widened and his mouth dropped open. "Oh, we are going to need a round of shots. Damn, girl, I'm kind of jealous of your Italian sex fest now."

I giggled. It was definitely worthy of envy. I left out the part about him tying me up and how big his dick was. I had to save some secrets for myself. "You should be. It was epic," I teased.

Three martinis and two rounds of sambuca shots later, my head was spinning. "Let's get some air. Wanna walk through Central Park? I still haven't seen it at night."

Max nearly choked on his last martini olive. "Are you for real? Do you wanna get mugged?"

I laughed so loud, I snorted. "Max, it's barely 8 PM. I think we'll be fine."

Max shook his head. "No, I have a better idea. Let's go check out the new speakeasy in Grammercy. I heard they are having a burlesque show tonight."

I groaned and reached for my purse. "You know how long that line is going to be. I hate lines."

Max hopped up off the bar stool and twirled me around. "Good thing I know the door guy. He already put us on the list."

"Okay, stop spinning me or I'm going to puke all over you. Fine. Since it's clear you pre meditated this, how can I refuse?" I was definitely feeling this buzz. Why not keep it going?

The brisk walk and fresh air did wonders for the dizziness. Six blocks later, we waltzed up to the front door of Cherry Juice and just as Max claimed, we were on the list and let in immediately. It was a good thing he had pull because the line was wrapped around the block.

Inside, the music pulsed against the melodic voice of a scantily clad singer. Her ruby red hair was pinned in curls to her head like something out of a French Noir film. She wore a colorful beaded bustier and a short poufy skirt. Short enough that it revealed her black lace garters and thigh highs. Six inch black stiletto pumps with red soles completed the look—a shade of red that matched her lips.

"Wow, this place is awesome," I yelled over the music.

Max grinned wide. "Right? I told you. You know I'd never take you anywhere less than fabulous."

We slinked our way through the crowd to get to the bar and ordered two old fashions. The chiseled bartender, wearing only black pants and a bow tie—no shirt—hand crafted the drinks in front of us using blood oranges, Italian cherries, and dry ice to give the drinks a smoke effect. They tasted as delicious as they looked.

Max and I squeezed into a corner booth near the stage to get a better view of the show. I was mesmerized by the singer in front of us. The sway of her hips seemed to match the rasp in her voice as if she lived on a diet of whiskey and cigarettes. And it was sexy. The only type of entertainment in Maplewood was either karaoke nights at the Rusty Nail, or the sad pathetic cries, falsely advertised as love songs, from Miller Wyatt, busking in the town square.

As Max murmured in my ear about having to use the bathroom, I spotted a familiar blonde, making her way over to our table. As soon as Max wandered off, she approached.

"Raven is it? So lovely to see you again. We met at Ozi's party a few nights ago." Camille. The mystery woman who got under Ozi's skin and disappeared shortly after he pulled her aside to discuss "business."

"Yes, I remember. Nice to see you again too."

Her skin was flawless, suggesting she was around my age, but the layers of emotion in her eyes reflected someone older. It was impossible to tell.

"May I join you?" Camille asked.

"Well, actually my friend will be right back."

The way she slithered into the booth ignoring my response let me know that she wasn't going to take no for an answer.

I scooted over so that I could face her directly instead of being nestled against her side by side. "How long have you known Ozi—I mean Mr. Fabiano?"

Her red stained lips curled into a smirk. "It's okay, Raven. You don't have to put on an act. I saw the way he looked at you. Anyone with half a brain can see that you two are sleeping together."

I nearly choked on my drink. "Is it that obvious?" I stammered.

Camille rested her hand over mine. "Relax, dear. I, of all people, understand the magnetic pull to that...man. He has a way of making every woman feel like they are the only one in the room. Trouble is, there's always another woman in the room. Just be careful. I'd hate to see you end up like me."

I jerked my hand away from hers. "What are you implying? Were you two together?" I was suddenly feeling out of my league, realizing this drop dead gorgeous woman had to be one of Ozi's exes.

"Yes. A long time ago. I don't like to talk about it often." She dipped her eyelashes down and stared into her dirty martini.

My curiosity was piqued. Between the way he manhandled her at his party to the sad look on her face now, I had to know more. I had to know who I was getting involved with. "I don't mean to pry, but can you tell me what happened?"

"I trusted him and he betrayed me," she spat.

"He cheated on you?" I asked a little too loudly. A couple patrons turned their heads in our direction for a split second before going back to their conversations.

Camille studied my face for a minute before letting out a sigh. "Sadly...yes. He is not the one woman type, Raven. If I were you, I'd reconsider spending time with him. He is sexy and charming and extremely good in bed, but he will only break your heart."

I felt crushed. Like someone knocked the wind out of me. Maybe she was just jealous? Maybe she was lying? "Well, thanks for the heads up. You should probably go. My friend will be back any second."

She smiled and nodded as she slid out of the booth. "I know it's none of my business, but next time you see him, ask him about me. His answer will be all the truth that you need. Ask him if he betrayed me." She turned to leave but stopped, turning back around. "Oh and Raven, if you ever want to leave *Dolce Sale*, I can offer you a position at my new restaurant. I'd love to have someone as talented as you on staff." She tossed a business card at me before strutting off.

When Max came back twenty minutes later, I had polished off two more old fashions. "What took you so long?"

He groaned. "Aside from the line to the restroom being a mile long, I ran into an ex on the way out. Sorry, girl. What did I miss?"

"Exes must be the theme of the evening," I replied curtly.

Max's eyes widened and he began looking around. "Your ex is here?"

"No. Not mine. Ozi's. The blonde from the party the other night. She took it upon herself to issue me a warning."

Max signaled to the server for another round. "Ooh spicy. Did she try to stake her claim on him or something? Tell you to back off? I love a good catfight."

I rolled my eyes at him. "No. Quite the opposite actually. She said he cheated on her and that I should stay away from him. Then she offered me a job."

"You should talk to Ozi. Look, I know he's a player. Always has been. But players don't usually commit themselves just to cheat. They don't have to commit to begin with. And the way Ozi looks at you, well, it's pretty obvious that he's into you."

"I hope you're right because I just can't get involved in a situation like that again. I'm still barely recovering from Alex. My heart can't take anymore breaking." The singer had slowed it down and was now crooning into the mic about unrequited love and lost chances. Between her voice and the multiple old fashions I'd consumed in the past hour, I had to fight the urge to cry.

Max squeezed my hand. "Talk to him before jumping to any conclusions. He might surprise you."

I blinked back tears and scolded myself in my mind for being so emotional. No one wants to be the sad crying girl at the bar.

"And as far as the job offer, you better not even think of leaving *Dolce Sale*. If you're not there, Tori will start picking on me again," Max teased.

"Oh, so I'm your human shield? Nice to know I'm appreciated for something," I joked back.

"You know I love you, girl." He winked and sucked down the rest of his drink.

I tried my best to push Camille out of my mind for the rest of the night, but her voice lingered in the back of my mind. Ozi was super secretive and he had women throwing themselves at him all the time. Not more than two weeks ago, I waited on him and that busty blonde that couldn't keep her hands off him. Did I really expect him to change his ways for me? Or was Camille right? Was I just another notch on his belt?

Nineteen

Ozi

MAPLEWOOD, CONNECTICUT WAS EVEN SMALLER THAN I HAD pictured. The welcome sign we passed declared a population of three thousand. It was no wonder that Raven was like a fish out of water in New York City.

Cassius typed away on his laptop as I sped through the woodsy terrain. "I'm not sure what I'm looking for exactly. Maybe it's just a coincidence that the hacker was in Maplewood?"

I gave him a long sideways look. "Seriously? It's also really fucking weird that her parents didn't see anything wrong with her sister marrying her ex. I can't put my finger on it, but there's something not right about any of it."

Cassius shut his laptop with a bang. "So they're a dysfunctional family. You've just described every human we've ever met. I still don't get why you're so keen on digging around. What do you think you're going to find?"

I gripped the steering wheel tight enough without snapping it off. Even after all these years, I had to remind myself of my own strength. "Well, hopefully more about this hacker. But aside from that, I like Raven. I want to pursue something with her. It's been a long time since I've even entertained that with a woman. But something is off. Trust me. If I let her into our world, I need to know that she won't be in any danger."

Cassius nodded. "Well, I did some digging into her internship. I wanted to see how she was selected and how she was able to afford the plane ticket to Italy. But there was no record of it. She claims she was at your winery in Italy and she clearly has an extensive knowledge of wine, but there's no actual record of her being there."

Fuck. "Okay. I'll ask her about it when we get back. I'm sure there's a reasonable explanation." Maybe she borrowed money from a friend?

Cassius groaned and lit up a cigar. "Fuck, Ozi. You're starting to sound like Lux." He puffed smoke circles in perfect rings toward the windshield.

I opened the sunroof to get some air. "What happened with Lux was different and you know it. That's not going to happen to me. Raven is nothing like Lilith or Camille for that matter." Lux was an incubus—a demon who feeds off of sex—and Lilith was his maker. She made him fall in love with her and then abandoned him. He shut off his emotions and has kept them off ever since.

I pulled into a parking spot in front of the Rusty Nail. In my two hundred years on this planet, I'd learned a handful of things that stuck with me. One of them was if you wanted information on someone or something, it was probably wise to ask the bartender.

Cassius and I stood out like sore thumbs as we exited my hundred thousand dollar black sedan in our three piece suits. The Rusty Nail was exactly what it sounded like—dark, dingy, and crawling with nosy locals that didn't take kindly to outsiders. They drank us in, scanning us from head to toe as if we had just come to steal their first born children.

I wiped the crumbs off a bar stool with my silk handkerchief and took a seat. Cassius did the same but only half-sat, keeping his eyes glued on the perimeter behind me. His wild streak would not allow him to be comfortable anywhere. Not in human spaces at least.

The stocky bartender, wearing a red flannel shirt and dark denim jeans, leaned against the wall, and glared at us. "Just passing through?"

I unbuttoned my collar. "Something like that. We'll take two shots of your finest whiskey."

The bartender moved slow toward the bottles. He slammed two shot glasses down in front of us and poured out something that looked like dirty water. "Fine isn't something we carry around here. This is what we got."

I knew I should have brought my flask. Something told me he had better booze but wanted to make sure we didn't stick around. "*Saluti.*" I lifted the glass to my lips and downed it back before I could gag. Cassius didn't touch it.

The bartender exchanged a chuckle with another patron, a squirrely guy who looked like he hadn't bathed in days. "What brings you through our neck of the woods?"

I smiled, tight lipped. "I'm glad you asked. I'm doing some research on the town and its prominent families. I was hoping you could tell me about the Monroe farm?"

He chewed on a toothpick, tossing it back and forth across his chapped lips. "What kind of research? You one of those big city detectives or something?"

"No, on the contrary. I'm a professor. I teach history. Thought I'd focus on small towns this semester." It was so easy to lie to them. Humans would believe anything to suit the narrative in their heads. Especially the one that removes any possible threat.

The bartender leaned back against the register, folding his arms to his chest. "The Monroe farm is just up the hill. Nothing much to tell. They keep to themselves."

Cassius picked up his glass finally and sniffed it before knocking it back. "How long have they been in Maplewood?" he asked, his voice gruff.

The bartender shrugged. "Long as I can remember. Not much of them left though. They got a couple daughters. One moved away to a big city I heard. The other one won't even go to the store by herself."

Nothing new. "Anything unusual about them?" I persisted. There had to be something.

The bartender looked up at the ceiling and scratched his chin. "Not that I reckon. Unless you count how their oldest one looks nothing like the rest of them. Rumor had it, she was the milkman's daughter if you catch my drift?" He winked and chuckled.

Now we're getting somewhere. "Oh? Go on." I placed a hundred dollar bill down on the bar.

His eyes lit up. "Yeah. I remember now. When Mrs. Monroe was pregnant with her, we never saw her. Not once. Mr. Monroe wouldn't let anyone inside their house for nine months. When she finally came out, the kid looked older than a newborn."

"And nobody asked or questioned them?" I asked.

The bartender shrugged again. "Not our place. They are a respectable family. And we mind our business around here."

I slapped another hundred on the bar. "Well, thank you for your time." I gave a Cassius a nod.

"You ain't a professor, are ya?" The bartender swooped up the hundreds just in case I changed my mind.

He wasn't the sharpest tool in the box but he was smarter than I'd given him credit for. "Have a good day." I smiled and gave him a nod before walking out.

As I pulled the car out of the parking lot, Cassius had his laptop open again, furiously typing away on it.

"Are you thinking what I'm thinking?"

Cassius didn't break eye contact with the screen. "That she was adopted? Yeah. I was searching the wrong databases before."

"You're still not going to find anything. You heard the man. Her mom hid inside to disguise the fact that Raven was adopted. It wasn't legit. There's not going to be a record of the adoption."

Cassius looked up. "So what are you saying? That she was stolen?"

"Or left on their doorstep. Either way, it explains why they have very little love for her. *Bastards.*"

"So what does any of this have to do with you?" he asked.

I shook my head. "I don't know. Maybe nothing. But I highly doubt this family would have been willing to pay Raven's way to Italy just so she could learn about wine. Check the winery records again. I want a complete list of everyone who was staffed at the time Raven was there."

"You got it."

As Cassius clicked away on the keyboard, I drove toward the direction of the Monroe farm. I had to see this family for myself.

"Oh, shit," Cassius said.

"What?" My heart was racing.

"I found something. Pull over," Cassius commanded.

I nestled the car on the shoulder. "What is it?"

"While there's no record of Raven as an intern that summer, there was a plane ticket bought in her name, round trip to Italy."

"Bought by who?" I snapped.

"Oh, fuck. You are not going to believe this."

"Tell. Me. Right. Now." The tips of my fangs were pushing through my gums.

Cassius used the back of his hand to wipe the sweat off his brow. "It was…Enzo."

What the fuck?

I shifted out of park and continued driving. A thousand dark and paranoid thoughts raced through my mind. I was too frazzled to even speak them aloud. Why would Enzo buy Raven a plane ticket to Italy and not tell me about it? But more importantly, why would he keep her name off the record?

The maple tree lined road curved as we climbed up the hill to the farm. I pulled into a shady spot under one of the trees and killed the engine. As I thought about everything—Enzo, the Monroes, how they treated Raven—a rage that I'd buried deep clawed its way to the surface. There was also the issue of the hacker and if any of it was tied together.

My gloved fingers tightened around the steering wheel. I stiffened further at the touch of Cassius's hand on my shoulder. "Are you about to do what I think you're going to do? I'm fine with it, but just let me know so I can clean it up quick."

I released a long drawn out breath, feeling my muscles relax and loosen as I did so. "No, I'm not going to hurt them." I murmured. "But I want to."

Cassius ran a hand through his long dirty blond hair. "Maybe Enzo has a good explanation."

"For lying? No. Fuck that. I will deal with him when we get back. I've given him everything, including my trust and loyalty. I expected the same from him."

"That still doesn't explain anything. Why would he take an interest in this girl? Why keep it a secret?"

"That's what we're going to find out." I jerked the car door open and jumped out. It was time to pull out all the stops and get to the bottom of this. "Wait here. They'll feel less threatened if it's just me."

"I'll be here if you need me. Try not to lose your temper, please. I really like this suit."

A gray-haired woman answered the door within four knocks. "Can I help you?" She looked me up and down the same way the bartender had at the Rusty Nail.

"I hope so." I clenched my jaw and reminded myself to stay calm. I needed to know the truth more than I needed to punish them. "I'm here about your daughter."

Her eyes narrowed at me. "Meadow ain't here right now. What do you want with her?"

I chuckled and did my best not to show my annoyance. "Your *other* daughter. Raven. I have a few questions."

Mrs. Monroe wiped her hands on her apron. "Is she in some kind of trouble? We haven't heard from that girl in weeks."

Shocking. "She's very ill. In fact, she may need an operation. I'm here to find out more about her medical history. Maybe even run some tests on the rest of you so I can get a better picture of her genetic makeup."

"Ain't you kind of young to be a doctor?" She eyed me skeptically.

I flashed her a warm smile. "I'm flattered, but I'm much older than you think. Now, what can you tell me about your family's medical history?"

Mrs. Monroe shifted back and forth on her feet, tapping against the doorframe with her nails. "How sick is she?"

I had to go full board on this one. "It might be fatal. She has a rare disease that we know very little about. Anything you can offer would be appreciated."

She chewed on her lip. "Look, mister, there's not much I can help you with. She ain't really mine. I'd appreciate it if you didn't say anything to Raven. She doesn't know. Wouldn't want to put that added stress on her with the sickness and all."

That was easy. She really didn't care for Raven. I could see the disdain in her eyes. Blood or not, she raised her. How could she not have one ounce of love for her? "Well, this is an interesting turn of events. Any idea how we can get in contact with her birth parents?"

She shook her head. "She was left on our doorstep with a note that said to never look for them. Someone wanted her hidden. I didn't want to keep her but my husband was getting tired of me not being able to get pregnant. So we took her in. A couple years later, my miracle baby, Meadow was born. Sorry I couldn't be much help."

"Oh you've helped plenty. By any chance...do you still have the note?" A gut feeling wrenched in my stomach.

"Yeah, hang on a second." She disappeared inside and left me standing on the porch. After ten minutes or so of me fixating on a broken shard of glass that stuck out of the lamppost, she emerged with a crumpled piece of paper.

I could feel the color draining from my face. "May I keep this?"

"Sure. To tell ya the truth, I don't even know why I kept it. Maybe as a reminder of just where she really came from." Her face was hard, weathered by decades of outdoor physical labor.

I turned to leave but something stopped me. I just couldn't walk away. I spun around. "Aren't you even the slightest bit concerned? You did raise her."

She avoided my gaze and stared out into the valley. "There was something not quite right about that girl. I knew it from day one. She ain't one of us. Never was. Now you best get on your way before my husband comes home with his shotgun."

For a split second, I wanted to show this miserable woman what a real weapon was. That her silly little shotgun was no more deadly to me than a toy. I imagined the look on her husband's face when he pulled up to find his wife bleeding out. The look of anger then fear and shock when he realized his bullets wouldn't work on me. And then finally, the look on his face when my demon face was the last thing he'd see before he died. In a quick moment, all these thoughts flashed through my mind and left.

"Today's your lucky day, mam." She opened her mouth to speak but nothing came out. Confusion froze on her face. I stuffed the note in my pocket and left without a glance back.

Cassius raised an eyebrow at me as I got back in the car. "Well?"

I handed him the note. "Raven was left on their doorstep when she was a baby with a pile of cash and this note…"

Cassius drew in a sharp breath as he read it. "Shit…the signature. Deveraux. But this means—"

"That Raven is a descendant of Camille's and her real parents are either dead or vampires." Suddenly the world felt like it was getting smaller and closing in on me. I loosened my tie and took a deep breath.

Raven was in more danger than I thought.

Twenty

Raven

I WOKE UP TO THREE MISSED CALLS FROM OZI AND ONE FROM MY mother. No messages. I hadn't heard from her since I left Maplewood and I hadn't bothered to call either. I sent her a quick text when I first got here to which she never replied. She was probably calling to make sure I didn't show up to Alex and Meadow's wedding. Wouldn't want the ex-girlfriend messing up her favorite daughter's precious day.

I groaned as I kicked my feet out of bed. I had an old fashion hangover and a bad taste in my mouth from my encounter with Camille. I started to dial Ozi back when I got interrupted by a knock on the door. A knock that quickly turned to banging as I dragged myself toward it.

"Raven, you in there?"

Ozi.

Shit. I was hungover and looked like crap. "Give me a second," I yelled through the door. I scrambled around to find my robe. Ducking into the bathroom, I splashed some water on my face and combed my hair up into a top knot. I dabbed some concealer under my eyes and swiped on a couple coats of mascara. We were definitely not in the stage of our relationship where I felt comfortable letting him see me like this.

A few minutes later, he was practically breaking in the door. "Hold on. I'm coming," I yelled.

I pulled open the door and found a very disheveled Ozi standing in the entrance. "I've been calling you all morning."

"I was sleeping. Sorry. Where's the fire?" My head was pounding and I was in no mood for his arrogance.

"Raven…I don't know how to tell you this, but I think you might be in danger. When you didn't answer your phone, I assumed the worst."

He wasn't making any sense. "What are you talking about? Why am I in danger?"

"Raven, I have a lot of enemies. Those who want to hurt me. Enemies who might fuck with you to get to me. There are other things you don't know. Things about your family—"

"*My family?*" I snapped. "You are starting to really freak me out, Ozi. What is going on? Tell me you're not doing some illegal shit." His pacing was making me nervous and the tone of his voice was unhinged.

He grabbed my wrists. "Raven, I just need you to trust me. I can protect you but I need you to come stay at my place for a while. I will explain everything. I will…show you everything."

How could I trust him when I barely trusted myself? "We can talk right here. I was willing to be patient with you but now you bring up my family and tell me that I'm in danger. You sound crazy. Especially after what Camille told me…"

His eyes widened. "You talked to Camille?"

"She approached me." Better to just rip off the bandage.

"Where? What did she say? What did she want?"

"At a bar. You failed to mention that she was your ex. She said you betrayed her. Did you? Did you cheat on her?" I wanted to hear him say it if it were true. I really wanted it to not be.

His eyes darted around. "Yes. No. I mean, it's not what you think."

"She warned me to stay away from you. Tell me she's just a bitter ex-girlfriend and that there's no truth to what she said."

He froze. Something flickered in his eyes—rage mixed with sadness. "I can't. But Raven you need to understand something. Camille is dangerous. There are things you don't know about us. That's why I need you to come with me."

He moved toward me, but I backed away. "You know how I feel about betrayal, Ozi. You know how broken I've been since Alex did what he did to me. I can't go through that again." I was shaking.

"It wasn't like that. I would never do that to you. You have to believe me." His eyes were sincere but then again so were Alex's every time he'd told me he loved me. "I'm a lot of things, Raven, but I'm not a cheater. I'm far from perfect, far from anything you have ever seen, but even demons have lines they won't cross."

I wanted to believe him. I wanted to run into his arms and forget everything Camille said. But he had so many secrets. And other than our obsession with ripping each other's clothes off, he hadn't promised me anything more.

"What am I to you?" I asked.

He slicked back his hair, turning away from me and toward the New York City skyline. "Something I wasn't supposed to have," he murmured.

"What does that even mean? I want to let my guard down with you but everything about you tells me to run away. Why should I stay?" I was done beating around the bush.

Ozi turned to face me, but kept his eyes averted. His demeanor changed. He was closing off, retreating within. "You probably shouldn't. Your instincts are right. I'm a predator, Raven. The worst kind. But the best way to protect you, to protect what we have, is by us sticking together."

My heart raced. "I don't understand."

He cupped my face in his hands. "I know. And I'm sorry for that. The truth is heavy and you may not be ready for it all at once. Please, Raven. Just come with me."

Every fear, every insecurity I had rushed forward. All the pain I tried to forget was back tenfold. Between his shady business dealings and his psycho ex-girlfriend, the secrets and lies would just continue. I was a fool to think Ozi and I could have anything different. "I can't do this again. Just go."

"Raven, *por favore*, please."

"Ozi, I said go." I bit my lower lip to keep it from trembling.

He nodded in defeat. "The old me would have thrown you over my shoulder and dragged you out of here. But I don't want to be that way with you. I will find a way to fix this, Raven. To fix us. Just stay away from Camille. I don't know what I'd do if anything happened to you." He squeezed his brows together, his eyes watery when they finally met mine, then turned and headed for the door.

I held my breath until he was gone. Once I heard the click of the door and his footsteps fade, I exhaled out and collapsed into a heap on the floor. And the tears came faster than I was ready for.

Ozi

The rain came down hard like shards of glass shattering against the roof of my car, streaming down the windows like blood. I closed the partition so I didn't have to make small talk with my driver. I pulled the brown leather flask from my coat pocket and took a swig. The taste of metal filled my mouth, sweet and bitter at the same time. The blood filled my veins, quelling my thirst, but did nothing to ease the rage that tore at my heart.

I wanted to tell her everything. That I was a vampire, that she was adopted and related to Camille. But she would have thought I was crazy. Or rejected me the way Camille had. I wasn't ready to turn her entire world upside down. For once in my eternally damned life, I did the right thing. The selfless thing. I let her go. If only she'd come with me... Maybe I would have had the courage to tell her more. It's hard to trust someone who doesn't trust you back.

The car slowed to a stop outside of *Dolce Sale*. Peering out the window, I caught a glimpse of Enzo at one of the tables, a glass of wine in his hand and paperwork spread out before him. I had trusted him, confided in him, and given him wealth beyond anything he could have ever dreamed of. This betrayal stung the most. It was beyond friendship. We were like family.

Cassius's words echoed in my head—*maybe he has an explanation...*

Maybe he did. But how could I ever forgive him for lying to me? For keeping secrets about Raven? I stepped out of the car, not caring about getting my thousand dollar suit wet, and walked inside my restaurant.

Enzo looked up, startled. "*Ciao*, Ozi. I didn't know you were coming by tonight. Everything all right?"

I clenched my fists at my sides. "That's the funny thing about vampires, old friend. You never know when one of us is going to drop by," I said through gritted teeth. "It's time you and I had a little chat about Raven."

His face paled as he went for his glass of wine. I knocked it away before he could reach it. Glass shattered at his feet. I slammed my hands down on the table and lurched forward, landing inches away from his face.

"Give me one good reason not to kill you right now."

Twenty-One

Ozi

ENZO COWERED IN FEAR. THE FIRST TIME HE'D EVER LOOKED at me that way. "Ozi, I was only trying to protect you."

"Protect me from what? I'm a vampire. There's not much I need protecting from," I snapped.

"Your heart. I was trying to protect your heart… Before you met Camille, she had other lovers." His hands were trembling.

This was going nowhere fast. "So? What does that have to do with me or Raven? Or you for that matter?"

He swallowed hard. "I—I kept tabs on Camille. I wanted to make sure she stayed away from you. Twenty-two years ago, I learned that she had a bloodline. A line of descendants. Humans. And the only surviving one was Raven. Camille was after them. All of them. So Raven's parents left her on a doorstep in Maplewood. A place that Camille would never think to look."

A twinge of anger was burning a hole in my belly. "Well, thanks to Cassius and an overly chatty hick bartender, I know all of that now. What the fuck, Enzo? Why would you keep this from me?"

"I didn't want to bother you with it. It wasn't a concern. The last person you wanted to hear about was Camille. I just always made sure she was far away from you. If I thought she was going to be a problem, I would have told you. It just didn't make any sense to worry you for no reason."

"What in the hell does that have to do with the internship at my winery?" I took another sip of blood from my flask. If I was going to kill him, it was not going to be from thirst.

"Raven applied for it on her own. I can't explain how or why other than fate. But she couldn't afford to make her way over to Italy. I felt for her. It wasn't her fault that she had been abandoned. That she was born from the Deveraux line. So I paid for the ticket and erased her name from the books so that Camille couldn't track her there. Even though they changed Raven's name to Monroe, I didn't want to take that chance. I had no idea she would end up here in New York City five years later."

My head felt like it was going to explode. "Enzo, she doesn't know anything about her own life. She doesn't know that vampires even exist. If you hadn't sent her to Italy, she'd still be safe in Maplewood." I would have never known her but at least she'd be safe.

Enzo hung his head and rubbed at his bloodshot eyes. "You of all people should know the world is a mysterious place. Maybe she would have found her way here regardless. Maybe it's in her blood. This attraction to you. She could have been seeking you out her entire life without even knowing it. Circumstances in her life led her here. It's not uncommon for a small town girl to want to move to a big city. Who knows? All I did was pay for her ticket to Italy. That's it."

I slammed my fist on the table. "How am I supposed to ever believe another thing you say? How can I ever trust you again? You know all my secrets. All of them. But you chose to keep things from me. Things I had a right to know."

"You have to believe that I thought I was doing what was best for you. I'm sorry. Did you tell her?"

I cursed under my breath. "No. She's been through enough. And I'm not ready. I have to find a way to keep her safe first."

Enzo's eyes filled with sadness. "Ozi, she's not like Camille. She may have her blood in her veins, but Raven is her own person. She will not hurt you. You must trust her with the truth. You're wrapped up in it just as much as Raven is. There's no telling what Camille's end game is. I know I told you to stay away from Raven before, but now I'm thinking you are the only one who can keep her safe."

Raven's blood. The first night I saw her, at my party, her blood…it smelled familiar. It spiked my thirst. Of course. It all made sense now. It was the same as Camille's. I needed to process all of this. Needed to figure out what to do next. "This conversation isn't over between us." I turned to leave.

Enzo stood up from the table. "What are you going to do?"

"Everything I can to keep her away from Camille. And you're right. I have to tell her the truth about what I am. Even if it means losing her."

The rain was falling harder as I made a dash for my car. I punched in Cassius's number and waited for him to answer.

"Cassius. How long would it take to put surveillance on Raven's apartment?"

"I already have it set up. Her roommate, Piper, is working with Lux. He had me install it months ago to keep tabs on her."

"Well, that's convenient for us. Okay. Keep an eye on her and let me know if Camille goes anywhere near there. I'm pretty sure she's stalking her. While we were in Maplewood, she cornered Raven in the city. Meet me at my penthouse in an hour. We'll figure out where to go from there."

"Shit. Okay I'll see you in an hour."

I hung up and told my driver to step on it.

I raced through the lobby and slipped into the elevator before the doorman had a chance to accompany me. I was in no mood for small talk and I needed blood. I didn't want to risk opening up one of his veins on the way up to my floor.

As I approached my door, I heard voices and loud music. What the fuck? I turned the key and pushed open the door to find my assistant, Charlie, doing a line of blow on my coffee table while three naked chicks surrounded him. One was jerking him off while the other two were making out with each other. Fuck. I did not have time for this. I was now cursing myself for giving him a key and for encouraging him to use my place for his sexual escapades.

Charlie whipped his head around at the sound of me slamming my keys onto the counter. White powder circled his nose. "Ozi! The party has started. I brought you some candy, boss."

"I'm not in the mood. Finish up and get the fuck out, Charlie." I went to my liquor cabinet and pulled out a bottle of whiskey. I poured myself a shot, downed it, then poured another.

One of the women, a hot blonde wearing nothing but a g-string, strutted over to me. She licked her lips and slipped her hand down my pants, wrapping it around my cock. As hard as she made me, she was not Raven. I yanked her wrist away and pinned it to the counter.

"Listen, honey, my dick does not belong to you. You do that again without asking and I will break your hand."

She flinched back, fear flashing through her eyes, but she laughed it off. "Suit yourself. You can just watch then."

She proceeded to climb onto the other chick who was spread eagle on my couch and began slithering up against her. Charlie watched as the third chick sucked him off.

I downed another shot and slammed the empty glass onto my marble counter. "Charlie, that's enough. You need to get out of here. I'm tired and I have work to do. I'll have my driver take you all wherever you want to go."

"C'mon, Ozi, play a little. You used to love my gifts."

My patience was dwindling and I didn't have time for this. "You have twenty minutes. I'm taking a shower. Be gone when I come back downstairs or I'll throw you off the terrace balcony."

I hustled up the stairs and came to a dead stop as soon as I reached my bedroom. A beautiful brunette laid naked in my bed. "I've been waiting for you, Mr. Fabiano."

"You need to leave. Hurry up, put some clothes on." *I was going to kill Charlie.*

She slinked around on my silk sheets like she was in heat. "But I'm your gift. You can do whatever you want with me." She arched her back into my headboard and pinched her nipples between her fingers, purring as she did so.

The old me would have ravaged her. The fact that Raven was the reason I could no longer even let myself enjoy this angered me. The naked woman on my bed angered me, teasing me with sex that I wouldn't allow myself to have. I grabbed her wrists and lifted her onto the floor. Raven was the only woman I wanted in my bed.

Raven

Before I could even process what had just happened, I found myself racing around my apartment looking for my clothes. The second he left, I knew I'd made a mistake. It only took me an hour of crying on the floor to realize that I'd pushed him away out of fear. He was begging me to come home with him and I panicked. While his talk of protecting me sounded crazy, I'd be lying if I said he didn't sound sincere. There was something desperate in his voice that made me think he was not overreacting at all. I needed to know the truth and if going to his place and hearing it on his terms was the only way to get it…well, I was willing to take that risk. Even if it left me broken again in the end.

Within twenty minutes I was dressed and hailing a cab in the rain. For the first time since I'd moved here, I didn't mind the way the taxi sped through the slick city streets. The faster the better. I had to get to him before I lost my nerve. The proverbial path I was on with him was uncertain, but it was the only path I wanted to be on.

The cab screeched to a halt outside of Ozi's building. I glanced up and saw the lights twinkling from his terrace. The doorman recognized me and made no attempt to stop me as I raced to the elevator and hit the button to Ozi's floor. Before the doors slid open I could hear the commotion. It sounded like a party. There was music, bottles clanking, and multiple female voices. A pit of dread sat in my stomach. I hesitated at his door, contemplating turning around and going home. But my curiosity got the best of me. That and the familiar feeling of jealousy. That same feeling I had when I heard the female laughter on the other side of Alex's office door. I was going to be sick.

I twisted the doorknob and to my surprise, it opened. I almost fell over as I took in the room. Naked women stretched and bent over his furniture, empty liquor bottles, white powder on the glass coffee table, and some chubby pant less guy hovering over the women. The guy was so strung out he didn't even notice me standing there.

"Where's Ozi?" I said louder than I'd planned.

The guy and all three women froze and turned their sights on me. "He's not here. You should leave." The man's gaze trailed upward toward the second floor.

I started toward it and he jumped in front of me. "Look, you don't want to go up there."

I avoided looking down at his erection and kept my eyes on his face. "Get out of my way." I tried to push past him but he blocked me. "Ozi," I yelled.

The guy grabbed me by the shoulders and nudged me back. "He's busy. Seriously, leave. You don't belong here right now."

"Take your hands off me or I'll scream."

Heavy footsteps raced forward, landing at the top of the stairs. Ozi stood there, fully dressed, but disheveled. "Raven. What are you doing here?"

I jerked away from the guy and folded my arms. "I came to talk to you about us. To tell you how I feel. I didn't realize you were throwing a sex party."

Ozi ran a trembling hand through his thick black wavy locks. "I'm not. It's not what it looks like. I mean it is, but it's not my party. I just walked in on this. I swear."

"This is your house, Ozi. Do you think I'm that stupid?" I was furious and humiliated and shaking so hard my teeth were chattering.

"I can explain. Charlie uses my place sometimes. Look, let's go somewhere else and we can talk." He started down the stairs when a lingerie clad brunette emerged from behind him and draped an arm around his neck. "Come back to bed, baby."

It was as if the air had been sucked out of the room. My chest constricted and I clutched my neck. "Oh, I have seen enough. That," I pointed to the woman, "explains everything. I'm done letting you lie to me."

"Raven, wait. I've done nothing with this woman. You have to believe me." He shoved the woman away, sending her a seething look at the same time. "Just wait, please."

Everything in my heart was hardening all over again, filling the cracks that he had managed to pry open. I wasn't just breaking; I was freefalling into a dark abyss where my emotions couldn't find me. Where love could no longer find me. "Camille was right. You betrayed me just as you betrayed her. I never should have trusted you."

I spun on my heel and leapt toward the door before he could catch up with me. Running, I slid into the elevator and frantically hit the button to close the doors. I could hear him calling out my name behind me. I caught one last glimpse of his dark eyes right before the elevator doors slid closed.

Twenty-Two

Raven

I RAN AS FAST AS I COULD UP FIFTH AVENUE, SKIDDING EVERY few feet as the rain poured down around me. In the near distance I could hear Ozi calling out my name. It was only a matter of time before he caught up with me. He was fast and my legs were starting to ache.

My apartment was too far to run to. I'd have to hail a cab or jump on the subway. But he'd no doubt follow me there. I needed to go somewhere he wouldn't find me. But where? I couldn't face him tonight. Maybe not ever. I knew from the start he was a player. I let him convince me he wanted to change. He told me I was different. Now I knew that was just a line he used to get me into his bed. I was such an idiot. After everything Alex put me through, I just wanted to believe that Ozi was a better man. But I was wrong. Again.

Shooting pain reverberated in my calf muscles each time my fee slammed into the pavement. It traveled past my knees, burning my thighs. My body wanted to slow down, to sit, but I had to keep going until I was far enough away from him.

It was late and the streets were half empty. Most people were smart enough to get out of the rain. Not me. I just had to run right into it. I passed cozy coffee shops and restaurants full of smiling faces and warm lighting. I could duck into one, but what if he followed me in and made a scene?

A red light forced me to stop at the crosswalk. *Come on, come on. Turn green.* Ozi's voice was getting louder, closer. I didn't dare turn around. I shifted my feet, transferring weight back and forth to bring some relief.

"Raven, please stop," he yelled.

The light was still red. Fuck it. I'm just going to have to run into traffic.

I stepped one foot off the curb just as a shiny black sedan pulled up. The window lowered and Camille poked her head out. "Get in."

I hesitated, looking back and forth between her and a faster approaching Ozi. I didn't know her at all and I didn't trust her, but Ozi was at my heels and I didn't have the stomach for dealing with him tonight.

She pushed the car door open. "Raven, let me get you out of here." Her gaze traveled past me.

I nodded and slid in beside her. I slammed the door shut and heard the lock click. Ozi threw himself at the car, screaming at me to get out. "Raven, what are you doing? Don't go with her. Please get out and let me explain everything to you." My eyes welled with tears as I raised the tinted window. Camille nodded at the driver and he stepped on the gas, lurching us forward so fast, Ozi stumbled backward, forcing him to let go of the car.

I sank into the leather seats. "Thank you."

Camille handed me a towel. "Of course. That's what friends are for. Shall I take you home?"

I scrunched my hair into the plush towel. "No. He'll be waiting there. Can we just drive around for a while?"

The corners of her red painted lips curled into a smirk. "Actually, I know a place we can go where he'll never find you."

I sighed and leaned back, closing my eyes. "Great. Take me there."

Ozi

My heart was racing. I ducked underneath an awning and furiously punched in Cassius's number. He answered on the first ring.

"Ozi, I'm at your place. Where are you?"

"I'm on the corner of 95th and 2nd. Tell my driver to bring you here. Now."

Fifteen minutes later I was in the backseat of my car with Cassius, speeding through Manhattan. I filled him in on everything that happened since we'd left Maplewood—my confrontation with Enzo, his revelation about Raven's ancestral line, Charlie's unannounced orgy at my penthouse, and chasing Raven through the rain only to watch her hop into a car with the very person I was trying to protect her from.

"How are we going to find her? She could be anywhere in the city," I grumbled.

"I've hacked into the streetlight cameras and am trying to piece together their route." Cassius typed furiously onto his laptop. "Take a left up here," he ordered my driver.

Each block we passed grew darker and more desolate than the last. It was three in the morning and while bars and clubs were still open, most other businesses had closed up for the night.

It didn't take me long to realize where Camille was headed. We were following her trail straight into the Meatpacking District. When the cameras showed her car slowing to a stop at a red light, Cassius was able to read her plates and punched them into his computer, giving us easier access to trace her on other cameras in the city.

"There." I pointed to a black sedan outside of an abandoned meat packing plant. There was a sign out front that showed plans for an office building with the words, *Coming Soon*, splashed across it.

The driver drove around the block and parked on a side street. "Keep the engine running just in case." He nodded and retrieved a handgun from the glove compartment. I didn't have the heart nor the time to tell him that wouldn't work on anyone who might be chasing us because they were vampires.

Cassius fell into step with me as we crept up the dark street, keeping to the shadows. We were predators. Hunters. This is what we did best. What we were designed for.

We found an entrance on the side of the building and made our way in without making a sound. I just hoped that we weren't too late.

Raven

I was starting to regret my decision to jump in Camille's car. She was right about Ozi never finding me here. What worried me more was that *no one* would ever find me here. It was dark, damp, and bare except for a few dusty pieces of furniture—a ripped velvet couch and a couple of hard wooden chairs.

Camille sat on the couch surrounded by four tough guys that looked like bodyguards out of some mafia movie. She crossed her long legs and dangled a martini over them. "I'm so glad we are getting this alone time, Raven. I have so much to tell you."

"Honestly, I don't want to hear any more about how Ozi cheated on you. I believe you. Can we please just talk about something else?"

She laughed. "Oh, I plan to. I didn't bring you here to talk about our piece of shit blood sucking ex-boyfriend. I brought you here to talk about you, dear."

Odd choice of words. An uneasy feeling washed over me. Everything about this felt wrong—the abandoned meat packing plant, the goons

accompanying her, and the way she eyeballed me like I was an appe-
tizer on a menu—it was all starting to make me think I was a prisoner
and not a guest.

"You know, I'm actually pretty tired. Ozi probably gave up for the
night. Can you just take me home please?"

"Klaus, bring our new friend a martini would you, doll?" The taller
of the goons nodded and ambled over to a makeshift bar on the other
side of the room. She narrowed her eyes at me. "We're not going anywhere, Raven. Not yet. Not until I've told you why you're here and my
plans for you."

Now I was really starting to worry. I reached around in my back
pocket for my phone, pulling it out, only to have the tall goon take it
from me and replace it with a martini.

"What is this? Can I have my phone back please?" I scanned the
room for exits but they were all blocked by more men.

"Did you ever wonder why your parents were so cruel to you?
Why they didn't love you as much as your baby sister?" She steeled her
blue eyes on me.

"How do you know about my family?" My heart was beating into
my throat.

"You were never supposed to be in Maplewood, dear. You didn't
belong there. But your parents were smart to hide you there so I
couldn't find you. Very clever of those two. Dropped you off at some
house full of country bumpkins so that I wouldn't be the wiser. But I
knew you would resurface eventually."

What was she talking about? Ozi had brought up my family too.
This was getting weird fast. "Look, I don't know what kind of sick game
you're playing, but you need to stop. I want to go home."

"It's not a game. It's the truth. Something that no one has ever told
you in your entire life. Those people who raised you were not your parents, Raven. They adopted you. Took you in because your real parents
left them a box full of money with the promise of more every year that
you remained alive and healthy. And your blood, the blood that runs

through your veins, is the same as mine. You are my family and I am yours. I'm your great, great, great grandmother."

My head was spinning, dizzying me to the point of almost passing out. "I think you have had a few too many martinis. You aren't that much older than me." *Or she was just batshit crazy.*

Camille stood and slinked over to me, twirling the olives in her glass while she strutted as if she were on a runway. "I only look your age but that's because you don't know what I really am. It will all make sense once you do." She snapped her fingers at one of her goons. "Bring her in."

I inched back. "What—what are you doing with her?"

Tori's blood shot eyes bulged as she struggled against her restraints. Her mouth was covered with tape. Camille pushed her to her knees. She grabbed a fist full of her hair and yanked her head back.

"This is my gift to you, Raven. This despicable girl has had it out for you since day one. Now is your turn to get payback."

This wasn't happening. I pinched myself, hoping this was all just a bad dream, but nothing happened. It was very real. "But I don't want payback. Please just let her go. Let both of us go."

Camille laughed. "Not until you see the truth." Her face began to change—her eyes darkened, shadows creasing across her face. Something strange was taking over her expression. Something dark and twisted. She pulled up her lips and two sharp fangs protruded out. She looked feral, like a wild animal.

I couldn't move, frozen in place with a fear I had never felt before. In one swift motion, Camille pulled Tori's head to the side and sank her teeth into her neck. Tori made a sound that was unnatural as Camille drank from her.

Oh shit, oh shit. She was drinking her blood. My heart was beating so fast and so hard I couldn't catch my breath. I was starting to see stars in my peripheral. *Calm down, Raven. Just breathe.* I couldn't pass out. I had to keep my wits about me. This was fucking insane.

Tori's eyes rolled back and her body slumped. Camille lifted her face and locked her feral gaze on me. Blood dripped down her lips, staining her chin. She smiled as she released Tori to the floor. She was dead.

Panic set in and my knees began to shake uncontrollably. "You... you killed her. Are you going to do that to me? Am I next?"

Camille wiped her mouth with a silk handkerchief. "No, my dear. I'm not going to kill you. I'm going to make you like me... Like Ozi."

The pieces were starting to come together in my head—the blood bags, the warnings of danger, all the secrets and the lies. Even though I already knew the answer, I needed to hear her say it out loud. "What are you? What is Ozi?"

Camille's grin grew wider. "Vampire," she whispered.

Twenty-Three

Ozi

W E WANDERED THROUGH THE WAREHOUSE'S FIRST FLOOR AND found it empty. But I could smell the blood. If I strained my ears, I could hear tiny, muffled voices coming from the upper level.

At the top of the stairwell, my suspicions were confirmed. Two of Camille's men stood guard. I motioned for Cassius to follow behind me and we crept up the stairs. Before the guards knew what hit them, we grabbed them from behind. I put one hand over his mouth and twisted his head, breaking his neck. Cassius mirrored my movements with the second guard.

"Look at the marks on his neck," I said, pointing to two fang marks just below the guard's jawline.

"Human blood bags. Clever." Cassius stepped over the contorted bodies.

Some vampires kept humans around to feed on. It was extremely risky as you'd have to make sure to know when to stop before killing them. The idea of Camille having any restraint was ludicrous but there they were. It was even more astounding that she had double downed and used them as guards as well. Unfortunately for her, this only made them easier to kill.

"Well at least this will be easier than I thought. Camille isn't that clever. Surrounding herself with humans when a vampire and a were-wolf are about to crash her party."

Cassius chuckled. "That bitch always was overconfident."

I found the door to the second floor and yanked it open. I almost dropped to my knees when I saw her. Raven was passed out on a velvet couch, one of my waitresses was dead on the floor, and Camille's face was covered in blood.

"Ozi, I was wondering how long it would take you and your pet wolf to find us. Welcome to Raven's rebirth party."

"What have you done, Camille?" I scanned the room and counted six human guards.

"Nothing yet, my darling. But soon your precious Raven will be just like us. Sad, tortured, immortal...famished for blood. And it will be all your fault because you couldn't protect her. Payback is a bitch, isn't it?" She stalked around Raven like a cat circling a mouse.

Cassius was breaking off from me while I had Camille distracted. He inched closer to the two guards at the other exit. But it wasn't the guards I was worried about. It was how dangerously close Camille was to Raven. Would I be able to get to her in time?

"Don't do this, Camille. Don't punish Raven just because you're angry with me. She doesn't deserve to have the choice taken away from her." As my hatred for her was growing, it was getting harder to believe I loved her once.

She bent down and ran her finger over Tori's neck wound, still oozing, coming away with a smear of blood. She licked it off, closing her eyes as she relished it. "Oh, Ozi, payback is really just the icing on the cake. As much as I love that this is killing you, it's more than that. Raven is my blood. My family. I have every right to turn her. There are rules in our world. You should know, you break all of them."

"I won't let you do it. If she wants to turn, it will be her choice. Family or not." I slid forward and charged at Camille.

Taking my cue, Cassius growled and whipped around the room like a bullet, dispatching the guards one by one with his bare hands, ripping into their throats with his claws.

Camille darted out of my reach faster than I anticipated. She laughed wickedly as we were now in opposite stances around the couch. "Can't even catch me in stiletto heels," she taunted.

Raven stirred, letting out a soft whimper as she came to. Her face was pale and clammy. Her gaze traveled from Camille to me, her eyes widening as she clearly realized the nightmare was far from over.

"Oh god. This isn't happening. Ozi, tell me she's a liar. Tell me she's crazy. Tell me…that you aren't a vampire."

I wanted to lie to her. To pretend this was just a sick joke. But I couldn't. Lying to her was how we got here in the first place. And she knew deep down inside it was all true. "I'm sorry, Raven. I was going to tell you. It was just never the right time. How do you tell someone you care about that you're a monster?"

A gurgle caught in her throat and she started dry heaving. I wanted to go to her and comfort her but I couldn't let my guard down. I had to keep my eyes on Camille.

"This is insane," Raven cried. "This can't be real…" Her voice trailed off into a whisper and she was going into shock.

Camille watched with a smirk, satisfied that she had just broken the one thing I loved the most. "Maybe she'll forgive you in time. Maybe not. I mean, look at me. It's been over a hundred years and I still want to ruin you for what you did to me."

"I'm sorry, Camille. I truly am. But we can't keep playing this game. It's time to end this once and for all." I nodded at Cassius, whom she had forgotten about in her frenzied obsession with me and Raven. He pulled up behind her and wrapped the silver chain around her neck. A chain that he always had on him. She gasped as it singed her flesh, paralyzing her in place. Raven screamed as I leapt forward, positioning myself face to face with Camille.

"I should have done this a long time ago. I am truly sorry for that. Goodbye, Camille."

She cried out, "Ozi, wait. Don't—"

I plunged my hand into her chest and ripped out her beating heart. I squeezed it between my palms until the beating stopped. Her eyes widened then went limp as the light left them, and a tiny tear rolled down her cheek.

I turned around slowly to check on Raven. She shivered, hugging her knees to her chest as she rocked back and forth on the couch. "Raven, it's okay. I'm not going to hurt you. Let me take you home." I crept toward her with my hands out in a submissive display. I didn't want to frighten her any more than she already was. But she still flinched as I got closer.

"Ozi, you need to get her out of here. I'll clean up this mess." Cassius was already starting to drag the bodies together in one pile.

I nodded and inched a little closer to her. "Raven, look at me. I'm going to take you home. Give me your hand."

She trembled as she began to move her hand toward mine. And like an idiot I forgot mine was covered in Camille's blood. Raven took one look at it and blacked out. I caught her in my arms before her head hit the floor.

I cursed under my breath. "It's probably for the best that you sleep anyway." I scooped her up in my arms and carried her to the car, leaving behind my past once and for all, but more uncertain than ever about my future.

Raven

Through the darkness, I could make out Ozi's shadow. I was in my room, in my apartment, and he was quietly sitting in a chair watching me. I ran my fingers across my neck in a panic. A sense of relief washed over me once I realized I hadn't been bitten. I pulled the cord on the lamp next to my bed and muted light poured through the room.

Ozi sat stoic, wearing his usual three piece suit, but the top buttons were undone. His hair was ruffled, matted slightly with a light sheen of sweat. His shirt was stained with blood but his hands were washed clean. He gripped the arms of the chair and stared directly at me.

"How are you feeling?" he asked casually, as if I'd gotten food poisoning and had not just been kidnapped by a vampire. As if I hadn't just learned that vampires existed.

My throat was raw. I reached for the glass of water by my bed and took a long sip. I wiped my mouth with the back of my hand, never taking my eyes off him. "How do you think I'm feeling? How would you feel if you saw two people murdered in front of you? One was drained of all her blood and the other had her heart ripped out. How should I feel?"

He sighed and leaned his head back against the chair. "It wasn't supposed to happen like that. I was going to explain everything to you. I swear."

I sat up straighter, crossing my arms. "Tell me everything. Right now."

There was an entire world that existed that I had no idea about. And apparently my life was tied to it even before I met Ozi.

"Let me pour us a drink first. You are going to need it." He went to the kitchen and returned with two bucket glasses full to the brim with whiskey.

As he handed me one, I couldn't help but flinch. It was a reflex. I knew I had nothing to be scared of. If he had wanted to hurt me, he could have done it weeks ago. And he did save me from Camille. But he was still a predator. And that terrified me.

He smiled and set the glass down on the bedside table. "I've been a vampire for two hundred years. I have no idea who made me. The last thing I remember was being attacked. Then I woke up on a fishing dock with an insatiable thirst for blood. It took me years to understand what I was. It took even longer to find people like me."

"And Cassius?" I asked.

Ozi stiffened. "No. He's not a vampire."

"But I saw how fast he moved…" I was confused more than ever now.

"He's a werewolf." Ozi stated it as calmly as one would talk about the weather.

This night was just getting crazier and stranger than I ever thought possible. "How many…things are out there?"

Ozi winced at my phrasing. "Many. There are witches, and incubi, fairies, and demons. Those are just the ones we know about."

Demons? "How could all of you exist and we not know about it?"

Ozi smiled. "Because we have a lot of money and we are good at pretending. And truthfully, adult humans only see what they want to see. It's much harder to hide who we are around children."

"You didn't make billions off of food and wine, did you? What else do you do? How are you all so rich?"

"We trade and sell things on the black market. We hunt magical artifacts. Well, Lux does most of the hunting, but the three of us— Lux, Cassius, and myself—own the business together."

I took a long swig of my whiskey. My head felt light and dizzy. "How many humans know about you?"

Ozi shrugged. "Not many. Enzo, a couple people on Cassius's payroll…your roommate Piper. She's with Lux now looking for something very important."

My stomach dropped. How in the hell did everyone around me know what was going on but me? "Piper? I must look like the biggest idiot. Here I am whining to everyone about my ex-boyfriend while you all are living in a real life urban fantasy novel."

"Don't ever think that about yourself, Raven. How could you possibly know? I didn't keep you in the dark to hurt you, I did it because I was afraid. Afraid that you'd look at me like you are right now…I also thought I was protecting you. Before I'd found out about your link to Camille. But I never should have waited this long. I should have been the one to tell you, not her. I'm sorry for that."

My curiosity was getting the best of me. "I have to ask… Have you ever thought about drinking my blood? How are you able to control yourself around it?"

He shifted his gaze to the floor. "Of course I have. It's in my nature. I can smell your blood from across a crowded room. I can hear your heartbeat over a thousand drums. From the first night I saw you at my party, all I wanted was to taste you… As far as controlling myself, well that's something that comes with time and practice. A new vampire would not have such control."

He was being so patient with me. So open. I had to know more. "Why did Camille hate you so much? She said you betrayed her. If you didn't cheat on her, then how? How did you piss her off so bad that she carried a grudge for a hundred years?"

"I'm the one who made her. I turned her into a vampire…against her will. Times were different then. I was different then. After I showed her who I truly was, she detested me. Threatened to turn me over to witch hunters. Lux wanted me to kill her, but I couldn't. I loved her. But I couldn't risk having her expose all of us either. So I had to make her one of us to keep her quiet." The pain and sadness in his eyes was heartbreaking. But the realization that I was now in the same position as Camille was a hundred years ago, chilled me to the bone.

I pulled the sheets in close, drawing up my knees to my chest. I couldn't stop the shivering. "Is that what you're going to do to me?"

Twenty-Four

Raven

MY HEART THUMPED IN MY CHEST. "TELL ME THE TRUTH, OZI."

"No. I'm not going to do that to you. I didn't think I had a choice back then. I believed we were in love, but when I revealed to her what I really was… Well, let's just say I didn't get the reaction I was hoping for. I had to protect my kind. I couldn't just let her run around screaming vampire to anyone who'd listen. Times were different back then. Witch trials were still rampant. I had to either turn her or kill her. Despite how she felt about me, I loved her too much to end her life. I realize now that I should have just walked away. I created a monster."

This was a lot to process. Supernatural creatures were real, I was adopted because my parents were trying to hide me from vampires, and now I was dating one. "What about my real parents? Are they alive? I need to know everything, Ozi."

He pinched the skin between his brows like he had a headache. Did vampires even get headaches? "I'm not sure if your parents are still alive. But if they died…they died as vampires. Enzo said you were the last human descendant of the Deveraux line."

I gasped. "Enzo? How is he involved in any of this?"

"Enzo is the one who paid for your ticket to Italy. He's kept tabs on you since you were a baby. He was so determined to keep you safe from Camille, that even I didn't know you existed." Ozi looked down at his blood stained sleeves, his face full of regret.

The weight of his words felt like a ton of bricks, crushing me into oblivion. "What happens now?"

He looked up and held my gaze. "That's up to you, Raven. I'm not going to force you to be like me. It's your choice. No harm will come to you if you choose otherwise."

Despite everything I'd learned about him, he still made my stomach flip and my knees weak. "I need time to think. To process all of this. It still seems…unreal."

He nodded. "Of course. There's no rush. I will give you some space to figure everything out. Again, I'm sorry for hiding this from you. I had no idea when we met that I was going to feel this way about you."

"What's it like?" I asked hesitantly.

"Being a vampire?"

"All of it. Drinking blood, being immortal?"

"It's strange at first. There's a thirst that consumes us. We learn to control it over time. Our senses are heightened. I can hear and smell things from a great distance away. We don't sleep. We can still enjoy regular food and drink but we don't need it. All we need to survive is blood. We must have it or else we'll die."

"How does one become a vampire?"

"You'd have to drink my blood after I drink yours. It would kill you like a poison but then you'd awaken reborn."

"Does it hurt?"

"Only for a moment. But it's forever, Raven. Once you become like me, there's no going back. There's no cure. Not one that I know of."

"Do you ever wish you were still human?"

"I used to. I wish I had been given a choice. But that kind of thinking gets me nowhere now. What's done is done."

While his tone suggested he was over it, his eyes hinted at regret. "How will you explain what happened to Tori? Enzo, her family...they will wonder where she is."

Ozi bit his lip and looked away. "I take full responsibility and I'm sorry you had to see her like that. I'm sorry for her. I will take care of it. Enzo knows the truth. Her family will be contacted and we'll make it look like an accident."

I was going to be sick. Images of her lifeless body, blood oozing out of her neck, came rushing forward. Was I still in shock? Even though my stomach was churning, I felt calmer than I thought I would be.

"I need to rest, Ozi. I need to be alone for a while." Truthfully, I didn't know what I needed.

He sprang to his feet. "Of course. I'll leave you to it. I'm sorry for all the pain I've caused you. That was the last thing I wanted to do to you. Regardless of everything, Raven...my feelings for you have not changed. Even if yours have. I regret not telling you sooner, but I will live with that mistake. You shouldn't have to. I will not blame you for wanting nothing to do with me."

I forced a smile but a part of me was still terrified. Judging by the look on his face, he saw the fear in my eyes. He looked sad, hurt, and disappointed. But I couldn't will myself to go near him, even though my body wanted to. My heart wanted to. But my mind was screaming at me to stay away.

"One more thing. I didn't lay a hand on any of those women at my penthouse last night. That was Charlie's mess. I know what it looked like but know that I never cheated on you. Since we met, you are the only woman I've been with. For what it's worth, I wanted you to know that too... Goodbye, Raven." He slipped down the hallway and out the front door before I could respond.

After a long hot shower, I bundled up in my robe and poured a huge glass of red wine. I needed to talk to someone but there was no one I could trust with this information. No one I could tell...except Piper. Ozi mentioned that she worked with one of his associates. That she knew about them. There was still this tiny part of me that was questioning everything. Second guessing what I saw and half-expecting Piper to think I was crazy.

I took a deep breath and another big gulp of wine and then dialed Piper's number.

"Raven! Hi! I was just about to call you and check in. How's everything going?" Piper's voice was chipper as always. I was beginning to wonder if that girl ever had a bad day.

There was something about the warmth and ease of her voice that sent me over the edge and I burst into tears.

"Raven, are you ok? What's going on?"

It took me a few seconds to get a hold of myself as the tears turned to sobbing. I choked on my own saliva and had to get a glass of water before I could form complete sentences. A few deep breaths and I was able to gain enough composure to speak.

"I know what he is, Piper. Ozi. He's a vampire. Tell me I'm crazy. Or tell me it's all just an elaborate joke. Please, this can't be real." My teeth chattered against my trembling lips.

Piper was so quiet. For a moment, I thought she'd hung up on me. "Piper, did I lose you?"

"No, I'm still here," she stated. "You're not crazy and it's not a joke. This is why I warned you to stay away from him. Once you know what they are, you can't *un*know it."

"How did you know this world existed?" I asked.

"I live in this world, Raven. I have for a very long time. It's my job. I hunt supernatural artifacts. I'm working with one of Ozi's partners right now."

"Aren't you scared?"

Piper sighed. "Sometimes. But I'm so accustomed to it now. I guess it's become normal. Raven, listen, unless you want to become like him, you should stay away. He's dangerous. All of them are."

I let out a slight whimper as I tried to stifle a cry. "I know. But I think I'm in love with him. I can't explain the hold he has over me. I've never felt this kind of attraction before."

"I get it. Believe me. But that's part of their charm. They're immortal which means they are physically perfect and have centuries worth of charisma they've been stockpiling. Of course he's never going to compare to a normal human man. I can't tell you what to do except to just be careful."

I hadn't even told her about my abduction or how I watched one of my coworkers get drained of blood in front of me. But at least I now had someone to talk to about all of this. That brought me some comfort.

"You be careful too, Piper. Thanks for listening. I'll keep you posted on what I decide to do."

We said our goodbyes and hung up and I was alone again. My apartment felt cold and empty. The more I thought about what Ozi was, the more I realized that it didn't matter. I didn't know if it was love or obsession or something else entirely. All I knew was that I didn't want to be away from him. Even if Piper was right and I was only drawn to him because of what he was, I didn't care. I craved him like he craved blood.

᠔

I rushed through the doors of *Dolce Sale* and nearly toppled Enzo over.

"Raven…are you all right?" His fingers trembled around a stack of menus.

"Ozi told me everything." I glanced around as some of the staff perked up at the mention of his name and then lowered my voice. "I know what he is."

He set the menus down. "Come with me."

I followed him to the back office. He shut the door behind us. "I'm so happy you are safe. I'm sorry you had to see all of that last night."

"Enzo…Thank you. For looking out for me all these years. For sending me to Italy. In a weird way, I feel like you're the only real family I have."

He clasped my hands in his. "I knew what Camille was capable of and I couldn't let her ruin your life. You deserved a chance to be human. Whatever you decide to do now, is up to you."

I wasn't sure if I wanted to live forever—an endless existence of drinking blood to survive. The only thing I knew for certain was that I wanted Ozi.

Ozi

The past could no longer haunt me. The only darkness hanging over my head now was from the shadows of regret. From losing Raven. I didn't even know how much I needed her until she was gone. How could she ever look at me the same again? She watched me rip out Camille's heart. She saw who I really was. And like Camille, she would probably reject me. The only difference this time was I would not turn Raven into a monster like me. I would not force her into this life. Unlike Camille, she had a chance at a better life. She'd despise me forever but at least she would still have her free will.

As the chopper took me back to my estate in the country, I looked over the Brooklyn Bridge one last time. I put my penthouse in Charlie's name and told Enzo to run *Dolce Sale* without me. There would be no more parties, no more women, and no more trips to the city. All I wanted was solitude. To be left alone with my guilt. The city held too many memories. All of my good memories of Raven were in the country. That one perfect weekend we spent together without any distractions from the outside world. I would cherish it always.

My phone rang, startling me out of my reverie. *Cassius.*

"I'm not in the best mood right now, just to warn you," I answered.

"I'm calling to let you know I took care of the bodies. None of it will lead back to any of us. Especially Raven. I also erased any paper trail of her going to your winery in Italy."

I nodded even though he couldn't see me through the phone. I breathed out a sigh of relief and anguish. "What about our hacker problem?"

"I've got a hold on that too. I was finally able to trace the IP address to an apartment in Brooklyn. Registered to a Harley Ryan."

I pinched my eyes shut, trying to fend off a blood migraine. "Never heard of him."

"Yeah, me neither. I'm putting a team together to retrieve him. Once I have the guy back at my compound, I'll find out who he's working for and let you know."

"Good. Use all means necessary to get him to talk. I'll be at my estate for a while if you need to reach me."

"Got it. Try not to beat yourself up for another hundred years over this one, buddy. Camille was coming after her regardless of you."

"I gotta go. Talk to you soon." I hung up before he could launch into another lecture about fate and destiny. His heart was in the right place but I just didn't have the stomach for it tonight.

As soon as we landed on my estate, I headed straight for the cellar and ripped open the biggest blood bag I could find. I sat in the dark and musty room on the floor, not caring about the dust getting on my designer suit. I stayed there all night. By morning, my shirt and tie were crumpled on the floor next to me along with three empty blood bags.

I jerked at the sound of tires hitting gravel coming from outside the main floor. I grabbed my shirt and flew up the stairs. I raced across the foyer and peered out the front window. It was one of my cars. The sleek black town car slowed to a stop. The driver jumped out and opened the door to the back seat. My heart sped up.

Raven.

Twenty-Five

Raven

STANDING IN FRONT OF OZI'S HOUSE, I WAS BEGINNING TO LOSE my nerve. Enzo had been kind enough to tell me where he was and to lend me the car. He'd said it was the least he could do for keeping me in the dark all these years. My heart was racing as I tried to think of what I would say to Ozi. How would this work? Would he still want me if I was only human? I'd age and he wouldn't. Would he be with me then?

The front door opened and he leaned against the entryway. His hair was disheveled, his pants wrinkled, and the first three buttons of his shirt were undone.

"You look like hell," I half teased, half meant it.

"You look stunning."

A rush of heat flushed my cheeks as he fixed his gaze on me. I had forgotten how sexy he was. How just one look could send me spinning.

I strutted forward in my little black dress and stiletto heels. It was the fanciest outfit I owned and he had not gotten a chance to see me in it. I stopped short of the porch, suddenly more nervous than I'd ever been around him.

"I've thought about everything you said and I've decided that I don't care about any of it. Not the money, not my job, not even the fact that you're a vampire. None of it. I only care about you. I don't know what that means or how any of this is going to work but I just don't want to be away from you. I know I'm just an ordinary human but—"

Before I could finish, Ozi flew toward me and scooped me up in his arms. His lips smashed against mine in a frenzy and I melted into him. His kisses deepened as I trembled against him. He worked the tip of his tongue around mine, exploring all of my mouth with a ravenous hunger.

"You are anything but ordinary, Raven. You are an explosion of stars lighting up my dark sky. You never have to be away from me ever again. I promise."

I kissed him harder and tangled my hands in his hair. The scent of tobacco and whiskey and blood filled my nose as the breeze picked up around us. His muscled arms held me tight to his chest and I let myself surrender to all of it.

He led me inside and began giving orders to his staff to prepare dinner. I stopped him.

"Ozi, I don't need anything fancy. Let me cook something for us." As much as I loved the way he pampered me, I wanted to pamper him for once.

He slid his arms around my waist, pulling me closer. "Darling, you're going to have to get used to people waiting on you for a change. I want you to have everything you desire." He nibbled on my earlobe.

My stomach did a little somersault. I gazed up into his eyes. "*You* are all I desire. Cooking is a big part of who I am. I want to share that with you."

He nodded, conceding. "I can't wait to taste every part of you."

Two hours later, we sat across from each other on the terrace under the moonlight. With just a few candles and twinkle lights, the glow illuminated the space between us like something out of a fairytale. I had prepared filet mignon in a red wine reduction, fingerling potatoes, and mixed veggies sautéed in truffle oil. I took the bottle of Bordeaux out of the server's hand and sent him away.

"See, isn't this more intimate? Just me and you," I cooed.

I watched his face light up as he chewed on the tender steak. "Oh, Raven. You have a gift. This is delicious."

My heart filled hearing those words, especially from him. "Thank you," I murmured.

Everything was new and scary and exciting. We both opened our mouths to speak at the same time and then stopped, laughing.

"You first," Ozi quipped.

I fiddled with the napkin on my lap. "I'm not ready yet to be…like you. I'm not sure if I'll ever be. I need more time to decide. Is that all right? I want to be with you for as long as you'll let me."

Ozi smiled and leaned forward, scooping up my hands in his. "Whatever makes you happy, makes me happy. You can be human for as long as you like. I will never take that choice away from you. And you never have to fear me. Ever. I will always protect you, Raven."

"What happens now? Do you want me to live here with you? Do I quit my job?" I was unsure as to what this new life would entail.

"You don't need to work as a server anymore. Everything you could ever want or need I will give you. I was thinking, however, that we could travel a bit. You *should* be a chef, Raven. And Europe has some of the best culinary schools and mentors. I could make a few phone calls and have you set up in days to start training… We could also try to find your birth parents. If you want to, of course."

My heart felt like it would burst. "I would like that very much. You would do that for me?"

"Raven, honey, I would do anything for you. I told you when we first met that I would break you…but it is you who has broken me.

In a way that I needed to be broken so I could be put back together. Only you could do that. For that, you have my heart in your hands for eternity."

He was right. I thought I was the broken one. The one who was weak and frightened. But it was my strength that held us together. I was lost and searching for him my whole life. I just didn't know it until now.

I was still scared. I had conditioned myself to hold back. I was so accustomed to keeping my guard up. But I was finally ready to let it all go. "What happens after I fall?" I asked. I already knew the answer but I wanted to hear him say it out loud.

Ozi pulled me into his lap and hugged me tight. "I'll catch you."

The End

Acknowledgements

This book has a special place in my heart. I wrote it during difficult times and it was a big part of what got me through. But it would not have been possible without the following people.

Thank you to my amazing editor and friend, Katie Golding. I started my journey with you back in 2017 when I was looking for a home for Blood and Magic. It was with your help that I was able to get that book noticed and it truly has come full circle with you editing After I Fall. I'm so happy you fell in love with Ozi and Raven as much as I have.

Thank you Sarah Paige at Opium House Creatives for creating the most beautiful cover I could ever dream of! You captured Ozi and Raven better than what was even in my mind.

Thank you Stacey Blake at Champagne Book Design for formatting my book with such skill and creativity. I am truly grateful I was able to work with you!

I have to thank Tina and Yelena of City Owl Press. You took a chance on me and have been so supportive of my career. No matter where my journey takes me, COP will always be my family and I look forward to releasing more titles with you in the years to come. Thank you to all my City Owl Press owls for your continued support and friendship.

To Negeen and Candace, We are such a fierce trio and I cherish our friendship so much. I love that we are always there for each other with writing and life stuff. I love our daily chats and I would not be able to get through this crazy thing called publishing without you. Love you both so much and can't wait till we can share a few bottles of wine together in person.

Thank you to my amazingly talented website designer, Cassandra Penticoff, for everything you do. You have helped me showcase my books and my ideas and I will forever be grateful. No matter what, you always get my vision and deliver it just as I've imagined.

To my mom, thank you for always supporting me, loving me, and being there through everything. I strive to make you proud every day. I love you so much and can't wait till we can take that trip to England together.

Thanks to my dad for everything. We have been in this pandemic together and I appreciate all you do to keep us safe, sheltered, and still laughing. It's been a crazy year but we are getting through it together.

To my sister Jen, I love you sis! Thank you for being my number one fan and for always encouraging me to keep going. I'm so proud of you and I can't wait to see what you create in the future. The Sercia sisters are doing great things.

Thank you to all of my family, Aunt Charlene, Uncle John, Kathleen, Marji, all the Sercias, Maioranas, LeFevres, Lyons, Driels, and Campbells. I love all of you and can't wait to see each and every one of you again.

To my BFF, Renee Infelise, thank you for friendship, love, and support over these past 15 years. Your words and encouragement get me through so much. Thank you to your lovely soon to be wifey Rachel for taking care of my bestie! I miss you both so much and I can't wait to visit you. I love you and am blessed to call you my best friend. Looking forward to more ComicCons, late night conversations, wine tastings, and silly shenanigans when the world gets back to normal.

Thank you to all of my amazing friends who continue to inspire me and bring a smile to my face every day: Brennan Kennedy, Joe Manuguerra, Julie Brooks, Katie Fisher, Serena MacLean, Ben Lawley, Art Lomboy, David Protelsch, Tatjana Papic, and Tiffany and Randy Werner.

Thank you to my new family at Spoiler Country Podcast! Your support is amazing and I'm so happy you've welcomed me in with open arms. Kenric, John, Jeff, and Casey: I'm learning so much from all of you. Great things are happening and they are only going to get more awesome!

Thank you to my reader community for joining me on this journey. I hope my books can bring you joy in times of uncertainty. To all the bloggers, I see you, I thank you, and I'm so appreciative of all that you do.

Last but not least, to my love, Christopher, thank you for always believing in me and supporting all that I strive for. This year has been insane and tough but I'm happy I can share it with you. All my love.

About the Author

 MELISSA SERCIA is an award winning Urban Fantasy and Paranormal Romance author with a passion for philosophy, mythology, and all things supernatural. She is the author of the *Blood and Darkness* series, *Beautiful Dark Beasts series*, and *Immortal Billionaires* series. Melissa lives in California with her man and her cat. When she's not building dark fantasy worlds and slaying demons, you can find her in the kitchen cooking with a glass of wine in her hand.

www.melissasercia.com

www.facebook.com/melissasercia11

www.instagram.com/melissaserciawrites

www.twitter/fluidghost

Made in the USA
Coppell, TX
31 October 2020